ZOMBOY

ZOMBOY

A NOVEL

Richard Scrimger

HarperTrophyCanada

Published by Harper*Trophy*Canada™, an imprint of HarperCollins Publishers Ltd

First edition

Harper*Trophy*Canada™ is a trademark of HarperCollins Publishers Ltd

HarperCollins books may be purchased for educational, business,
or sales promotional use through our Special Markets Department.

HarperCollins Publishers Ltd
2 Bloor Street East, 20th Floor
Toronto, Ontario, Canada
M4W 1A8

www.harpercollins.ca

Library and Archives Canada Cataloguing in Publication
information is available upon request

ISBN 978-144341-068-7

Printed and bound in the United States
RRD 9 8 7 6 5 4 3 2 1

To my son Sam, who thinks about zombies a lot

CHAPTER 1

WHERE DOES A STORY START?

It was the worst Tuesday of the year. You know the one I mean. I was going into grade seven at Westwood Elementary in my smallish town—Dresden, Ontario, home of the Buzzards of the Inter-County Football League. (Go Buzzards!) The sun was about to pop out from behind a fluffy cloud, the school bell was about to ring, and my pulse was running about 140 beats per minute because we were going to jump to our death.

"You have to, Bob," said Evil-O. "You said you would jump. Come on."

"It's a mile down!"

"Is not. Don't be such a chicken."

"Our bodies will smash on the rocks and the vultures will eat our corpses."

She smiled.

"I don't wanna," I said.

"I'll say one, two, three, and we'll jump. Ready?"

"No."

"Bob!"

"Hey, guys!" said Gezink. "What are you doing?"

His head was just below our feet. He was on the ground and we were standing on the bridge of the climbing thingy in the school playground. The sun popped out and Gezink's glasses flashed. His nose was running. Something was usually leaking out of Gezink.

"Jumping to our death," I said.

"Get out of the way," said Evil-O.

A few years ago Dresden was voted one of the top ten places to live in Canada, and the bit I could see from up here looked clean and green and nice. The September sky was dotted with spoonfuls of mashed-potato clouds. Dinky little trees stood on front lawns up and down Westwood Avenue like soldiers on parade. Mr. Buzminski, the principal, was smoothing down his hair with both hands. A few kids ran around the playground screaming, but a lot of them stood around looking sad. They knew what day it was.

"One, two—"

"Hey, look!" I said. "A school bus. What's it doing here?"

Westwood is a neighbourhood school. A couple of kids get lifts but mostly we walk or ride bikes or skateboards. The only time you see a bus is when you're going on a class trip.

"Bob," said Evil-O. "Pay attention. We're jumping."

"Geez, Evil-O. I don't think I'm ready to do this. I have frail bones, you know. I do—I just remembered. My doctor says I'm like an eggshell inside. The impact from a fall might—"

"One, two, three!"

She grabbed my hand and pulled me with her. I screamed. (Sorry. I mean, I gave a manly shout—*Death from above!* Or something.) We landed, and I rolled onto the pebbles that surrounded the climber.

I checked my body for pain. Little ouch in my left knee but that was all. Could have been worse. The three-legged race at the county fair last summer—that was worse. I ended up on crutches for three weeks. Evil-O's always getting me into things. Hanging out with her means living with danger. She's one of those JUST DO IT girls. On my own, I'm more of a THINK ABOUT IT AND THEN GO HAVE A SNACK guy.

Evil-O was on her feet. "That was fun!" she said.

I lay still.

"You're not really dead, Bob," said Gezink. "I can see you breathing. Your stomach's going up and down."

Mrs. Swartman came by and told Evil-O to be careful and me to get up.

"But it's the worst Tuesday of the year," I said.

"Tell me about it," said Swarty.

Evil-O and I met in kindergarten, the year she and her mom moved onto my street. Her name was Olive then. I told her that I could say my name backwards or forwards. Bob or Bob. I like it backwards best, I said. She laughed and said that she liked her name backwards too. It took me a minute to work it out, and then Olive became Evil-O. And she's been Evil-O ever since. Everyone except her mom calls her that. Every year on her birthday, the announcement over the loudspeaker says, *Celebrating a birthday today, Evil-O Forester.*

We grabbed her skateboard and our backpacks and went over to the school bus. Only one kid came out. At first I thought he was a first-grader, he was that small. Way shorter than me and even skinnier than Evil-O. Scrawny little guy. He wore a long-sleeved shirt, even though it was a warm day. Baggy pants held up by a belt.

"Hi there!" said Evil-O, super-friendly. He nodded *hi* back. His face was older than the rest of him. It had lines and creases and things. He looked like he hadn't slept in a year. Not a first-grader at all.

"What's your name?"

"Imray," he said.

"Nice name."

"Is it?" He sounded doubtful.

Before we could introduce ourselves, Mr. Buzminski came over and led him into the school, ignoring us completely. Evil-O shouted goodbye. I didn't.

"Something about that guy," she said.

"Yeah."

"He's kind of cool, don't you think?"

"No," I said. My knee was still twinge-ing. I rubbed it.

The bus was backing down the drive. I caught a flicker of movement from inside—something pressed against the windshield. Or some*one*. I grabbed Evil-O's arm.

"D'you see that?"

The bus backed onto Westwood.

"There it is again! See? Someone's inside."

"The driver?"

"No, something else. A face or—or something."

"You're dreaming, Bob."

The bell rang. Time to line up. Evil-O and I stood together. She clutched her skateboard in both hands. "I wonder what grade the new kid's going into?" she asked.

She seemed awful interested in him.

A kid ahead of us in line fell over. I heard Calvin's laugh. I bet he'd pushed her.

"What happened to you?" I asked Gezink. He was sucking his finger.

He shrugged, checked the end of his finger, and put it back in his mouth. He was that kind of guy, Gezink. Always catching bits and pieces of himself on things. "Most days I end up bleeding," he said once.

CHAPTER 2

Westwood is a small school. Our class has been together for years. We took our usual seats—Susan and Andrew at the front where they could answer the questions, Calvin at the back where he could pick his nose and hit whoever sat in front of him, Debbie and Dakota by the window so they could look out and be distracted, and Evil-O and Gezink and me in the row nearest the door. It might have been last year, only instead of Swarty we had Mountain Woman at the front of the class. I don't know who came up with that name for Ms. Eiger. She had white hair and brown dresses and her body got a lot wider as it went down. Like a mountain, right? She had a wheezy rumbly voice. Mountains don't talk but if they did they might sound like her.

"Good morning … class, welcome to grade … seven," she said. "My name … is Ms. Eiger as you … know *Calvin* … put down the pencil."

She kept pausing to take breaths. You never knew what she was saying until she finished, and sometimes not even then. Calvin had been about to poke Travis, who was in front of him. He sat back. Ms. Eiger's eyes glittered, a vein of meanness catching the light.

The announcements came on. Mr. Buzminski welcomed us back to school. We stood up for "O Canada" and had a joke for the day: Where does the king keep his armies? In his sleevies. (Yes it's dumb but it's kind of funny too.) Then Buz made a special announcement.

"Boys and girls, Westwood has a new student this term. His name is Imray and he will be in grade seven. I want you to be extra nice to him, okay? He has gone through a difficult time and is now ready to return to school and get on with his, uh, life. I'm going to give him the microphone. Can you say hello to your fellow students, Imray?"

Some bumps and bangs and then a new voice came over the loudspeaker. "Hello, everybody."

And that was it. Buz came back on and hoped we'd have a great day.

Evil-O turned around in her seat. "So that's why Buz was making such a fuss about him," she whispered. "The poor little guy. And now he's in our class. Isn't it great, Bob?"

Her eyes were soft with sympathy. Boom! Just like that, she was all over this Imray.

"'Difficult time,'" I whispered back. "What does that even mean? I've had my difficult times too. Remember those mysterious spots on my arms last year? They itched for days, and the doctor never did figure out what they were."

Evil-O turned back around.

A minute later the door opened and Mr. Buzminski came into our room with the new kid. Under the lights his cheeks looked even whiter than they had outside. It was like he was wearing makeup.

Buz wrote the kid's name on the board: IMRE LAZAR.

So that's how you spelled it.

Buz turned to face us. "Hi guys!" He gave us his best principal smile. "How you all doing? Welcome back. You're in grade seven now, the biggest kids in the school, and I am expecting a lot from you. You heard about Imre over the announcements. I want you to be nice to him. Can you all say hi? Come on now. Be polite!"

"Hi, Imre!" called Evil-O, clear as a bell. The rest of us looked away and muttered something, the way you do when grown-ups tell you to be nice. Susan, the teacher's pet, wore a cold smile. Calvin was drawing on the back of Travis's shirt with his pencil.

"There, you're all friends." Buz smiled. "Isn't that great?"

"Oh, yes, sir," said Imre gloomily. "I can feel the warmth."

Was he making a joke? I couldn't tell. Buz left. The silence stretched. The clock ticked heavily as the minute hand moved forward: 9:22. I checked my desk for candy. An old habit—I could usually find a stray caramel or jelly bean nestled among the notebooks and worksheets. Not the first morning of school, though.

Ms. Eiger asked Imre to find a seat. There were a few empty ones, but Evil-O waved her hand wildly. "Over here, Imre!" she said. "Sit here! There's an empty seat beside Bob."

9

Ms. Eiger glittered meanly again. She didn't like Evil-O. She was always telling her to stop running in the halls and to be quiet. Imre ducked his head, smiled, and took his seat next to me. Ms. Eiger started handing out textbooks. The class gave a collective sigh. Another year of school was starting.

Evil-O half-turned and introduced herself to Imre in a whisper. She nodded at me.

"And this is Bob Fuller. My best friend."

He reached out his hand and we shook, not happily on my part. You ever get that feeling—ominous, creepy, threatening? His nails were longish and dark. The skin was pale to whiteness and icy cold. Seriously yucky. I searched my backpack for hand sanitizer.

"Welcome to our school! I'm sorry about your tough time," Evil-O said.

Her face is thin and long and her jaw sticks out, dragging her mouth open so you can see her top teeth. It gives her a strong, serious look. Her dark eyes were full of sympathy.

Imre shrugged, playing it cool—or as cool as you can be when your feet don't touch the floor. I wrinkled my nose. Up close, he had a chemical smell. Like a science experiment.

"Well, I think you're very brave," she said. "And Bob does too, don't you, Bob."

CHAPTER 3

"What do you think happened to him?" asked Evil-O.

"Who?"

"Who do you think? Imre. What do you think his tough time was?"

We were halfway down Westwood Avenue, Evil-O on her skateboard and me trotting along beside her. Sunshine, leaf blowers, dogs with wagging tails, parents holding their little kids' hands.

"Can we talk about something else?" I asked.

I'd had Imre all day. Sitting beside him, listening to Evil-O explain things to him, eating lunch with him (and let me tell you that was a strain—my baby cousin, who put her head right into her last birthday cake, is a neater eater). Now that school was over I was hoping to get back to normal, talking about homework and TV and snacks and stupid stuff your parents do. Regular things. But Evil-O wouldn't let go of Imre. At the corner she leaped the curb, landed on her board, and steered down Ewing Street. She was pretty good.

"Don't you *like* Imre, Bob?" She turned to look back at me, afternoon sun behind her, hair ruffling around her face, eyes in shadow.

I didn't. Not at all.

"Imre's great," I muttered, "for a shrimp who smells weird and eats like a pig."

"What was that?"

"Nothing."

The rest of the walk home was pretty quiet. Evil-O was working on a trick where the board twirled in a spiral. She tried it a dozen times and kept missing. I watched her and felt a strange new low, like my life was changing right now, this minute. I didn't know how to stop it or why the change made me feel bad. So there was a new kid in class and Evil-O liked him—so what? She liked me too. She and I were still friends.

"You want to come in?" I asked when we got to my place. Hers is two doors down. "There are butter cookies."

I pictured them in their round tin on the kitchen counter, glistening with sugar. They called to me—you know how cookies do.

"Nah, I'm okay. I think I'll go home and look up Loewen County. It's up north."

"Oh."

Loewen County was where Imre came from. He'd told us at lunch. Now Evil-O was going to look the place up even though he didn't live there anymore.

I watched her skate away and felt my heart crumble inside my chest. I might have cried except that I heard a voice.

Bob. Bob.

A sweet voice whispering my name.

We're here for you, Bob. Come on inside, Bob.

Ahhh, butter cookies.

I knocked on Evil-O's door next morning and we went to school like usual. And the next day, and the next, and on through the following week. School was school. Bells and lockers and lunch boxes. Fractions and the water cycle and recess. Staying out of Calvin's reach and taking Gezink to the nurse's office for ice and Band-Aids. Ducking behind my textbook so Ms. Eiger would choose Andrew or Susan to explain the answer. Trying not to worry about how much time Evil-O was spending with Imre. Worrying anyway. Checking my pulse.

Imre turned out to be a pretty funny guy. He was so gloomy that I found myself laughing along with him now and then. Like when Susan was teasing him about his last name.

"Such an odd combination of letters," she said. "It's so . . . ethnic. How on earth do you pronounce it? Is it like *laser*?"

If she was trying to make him feel bad, it didn't work.

"It rhymes with bizarre," he said. "At my old school they used to call me Lazar the Bizarre. Pretty funny, hey?"

We were in the hall, lining up for something. Imre was behind Susan and ahead of me. I started to giggle.

"Go ahead, Bob," said Imre gloomily. "Laughter does you good."

Which made me laugh harder.

We weren't friends, though. There was something definitely *off* about him. And when Evil-O looked at him and her face got all soft and caring, I felt like throwing up.

I tried talking to my parents about it at dinner but my timing was bad. They were going to a poetry reading that night and they were running late. Dad served us at the kitchen table, standing behind us and reaching around to dump food onto our plates. Mom began eating while he was still serving.

"Do I have to like everyone?" I asked.

Mom was chewing quickly, eyes on the window, thinking about something else. I repeated the question.

"Oh, sorry, Bobby. Uh . . . yes. Yes, you should try to like everyone."

Beef stew is one of Dad's best dishes. We'd had it the night before too, but I didn't mind having it again. In fact, it was better the second night. The meat was tenderer and the gravy was thicker and the peas tasted like part of the stew instead of just like peas.

"Everyone?" said Dad, sitting down. "That's kind of broad. You don't have to like neo-Nazis or some mass-murdering psychopath. No real bad guys. I wouldn't even try to like them."

Mom rolled her eyes. "Bobby isn't talking about murderers, dear. He's talking—"

"Or that weatherwoman on the morning show—you know, the one who winks at the camera. As if there's something cute about the weather. I can't stand her."

14

Some of the dark sauce had spilled onto Dad's sleeve. He wiped it off with his fingers and licked them. Mom told him he'd better change his shirt after dinner, and he said it was okay. She said it was not okay, that she didn't want him going to the reading in a stained shirt. And he said he didn't care what Zibby Stinson and the Dresden poetry crowd thought of the way he dressed. And she asked if he cared what *she* thought. He said *umph* and took another bite of stew.

(Do your parents talk like this? Mine do. All the time.)

"See, there's a new kid in our class. I think he's creepy and I was wondering if I had to like him. Evil-O does. A lot."

I added that last bit with extra meaning, and looked up quickly from my plate. Had Mom and Dad heard the hurt in my voice?

They had not. Mom was asking Dad what he meant by *umph*. And he was saying he didn't mean anything by it. Just *umph*, he said. So you'll change your shirt, Mom said. And Dad said *umph* again.

"I don't want to hang out with the new kid very much," I said. "But I don't want to lose Evil-O as a friend. What do you think I should do?"

Dad was over by the sink, dabbing away with a tea towel. "Aha!" he said, holding up his dripping sleeve. "See, the mark's gone. Now I don't have to change!"

He smiled. Mom held her frown for a moment before turning to me.

"Sorry, Bobby, did you say something?"

15

I swallowed my mouthful. Man, it was good. My heart was messed up, but the stew was really tasty.

"Just wondering if there was any chance of seconds," I said.

CHAPTER 4

Evil-O's house is a lot like mine except that it needs painting. She called goodbye to her mom. Her mom yelled back at her not to forget her lunch. "And watch yourself, Olive. Know what I'm saying?"

Evil-O got her skateboard from the garage. I knew she hated her mom calling her Olive. I knew a lot about her.

The Day of the Piano (as I think of it now) was a chilly-ish one. I was wearing a sweater because I am susceptible to colds, and mine are Supercolds—they jump into a phone booth and come out as fevers with little red capes, and my temperature leaps tall buildings in a single bound. Evil-O was in jeans and a shirt that went down over her fingers. She laughed at my sweater. She isn't delicate the way I am.

We talked about breakfast and sunspots and Razor, the dog from around the corner on Ewing Street. Evil-O made a curb jump the first time she tried it. Her smile flashed like lightning in her tanned face. The dragonflies were out. They

17

were huge this time of year. When the sun hit them they looked like jewels.

The halls were busier than usual that morning. A bunch of moms and dads were going into Mrs. Swartman's classroom. She has this take-your-parent-to-school day at the start of the year. Mr. Foubert was in his firefighter's uniform and my doctor, Dr. Sophie from the clinic, wore her white coat. Her daughter Molly was in Swarty's class this year. Dr. Sophie waved when she saw me. I'm in her office a lot.

After the announcements we changed our shoes and headed down the hall to the gym. That's when we heard the rumbling. Our part of the hall slants up towards the office like a ramp and the rumbling came from above us. I stared in disbelief as the school piano appeared from around the corner, turned slowly, and headed straight for us. It was one of those old uprights—about the size of a couch. A second later the janitor appeared, waving his arms and yelling at us to watch out!

Runaway piano. You don't meet one of those every day. The thing weighed a ton and was rolling fast down the narrow hall, bumping from wall to wall.

We stampeded. No place to turn or hide, so the whole class just ran. The rumbling got louder as the piano gained on us. And then behind me I heard this heavy splintering jangly *crash*, like a wrecking ball hitting an orchestra. The rumbling stopped, but there were *jangles* and *twangs* and deep *sproing*-y sounds that echoed for a bit. I was puffing like a steam engine.

"Imre!" Evil-O screamed.

Oh? I thought. And then, Oh!

He stood in the middle of the hallway and the piano lay on the floor on both sides of him. The thing had split in half and fallen over in a mess of wood chunks and wires and piano guts. There were black and white keys spread all over the place. Imre stood calmly, lifting his feet one at a time and shaking them free of dust.

I didn't understand what had happened right away—and when I did, I didn't believe it. It was like Imre was walking away from a plane crash.

Calvin was beside me. Big Calvin, with muscles and body odour and meanness. His face was pale.

"Holy crap," he whispered.

Farther up the hall, doors were opening. Voices were raised. People were coming.

"Did you see that?" Calvin whispered to me. "Piano hit the new kid and busted. Just . . . busted right in half. Holy crap!" he said again.

Evil-O ran over and grabbed Imre's hand. "You're all right!" she said. "Are you all right? *How* are you all right?"

Good question. There was a piece of wire sticking out of his shoulder. It wiggled when he shrugged.

Blood was soaking Gezink's shirt sleeve. He'd been near Imre, and it looked like another wire had caught him in the arm. Poor old Gezink.

"A doctor!" Ms. Eiger called. "Is there a doctor in the . . . house?"

III

There was. Dr. Sophie checked us out in the nurse's office—all of us who'd been close to the piano. Gezink was the only one who needed a bandage. Dr. Sophie told the rest of us we could go back to class if we wanted.

My pulse was 135. "That's high, isn't it?" I said, and Dr. Sophie agreed, but she said that I was a nervous kid anyway.

"You mean sensitive," I said.

"Yes." With a smile. "Don't worry, Bob. You're okay."

She checked Imre again, even though he said he felt fine.

"The piano smashed into your back and yet there's no mark." A thin crease of frown ran up the middle of her forehead. "You should have been knocked down and hurt badly, but there's not even a bruise. It's very strange."

"I'm strong," he said. "For my size."

Calvin made a snorty noise on his way out the door.

"And there's no bleeding," the doctor went on, peering at Imre's shoulder. "That other boy was soaked with blood. You had a piano wire stuck right into you and not a drop of blood has come out. I can't believe it."

She put her fingers on Imre's wrist and neck and frowned.

"What's wrong?" asked Evil-O. She sat beside Imre. She wouldn't leave even though she was totally fine.

"I can't seem to find a pulse," said Dr. Sophie.

"*I* have a pulse," I said. "It was high, remember? Maybe you should check it again. I'm feeling a bit light-headed."

There was a thermometer in a bracket on the wall. When the doctor took Imre's temperature in his ear, the number made her eyes widen. She checked that the thermometer was working and took Imre's temperature again. All this time he was sitting on the bench in the small blue-painted room, hands in his lap, about as anxious as a bag of fertilizer. Evil-O told him not to worry.

"I am not worried," he said. "Nothing can happen to me."

Dr. Sophie was talking into her cell phone. The ambulance arrived five minutes later and Imre went to the hospital. I wasn't there but I know what happened. Imre got tested some more and his results were flashed to Toronto and Montreal and Atlanta and Baltimore and all sorts of other places, and doctors everywhere were as astounded as Dr. Sophie had been because the tests showed that Imre was, well, dead.

CHAPTER 5

How long did it take for this news to spread all over the place? About as long as it takes you to get wet when you fall in the pool.

"Here's a startling story," the CBC news guy told us the next morning. "An Ontario schoolboy has been diagnosed with something straight out of a horror film. He has no pulse, no blood pressure, and a body temperature just above freezing. With no vital signs, the boy, whose name is being withheld, is not technically alive, yet he is able to function normally. Doctors are completely unable to account for his condition, which has been named *pedes mortuus*, or 'walking-dead' syndrome. At this stage there is no reason to believe that the condition poses a threat to people who have been in contact with the boy or to the population at large."

There was a shot of our highway sign: WELCOME TO DRESDEN, POP. 17,500. No question that the story was about Imre. The news guy had serious hair and a chin dimple and he could flex his eyebrows like biceps.

This was breakfast time. Mom had gone to work and Dad and I were standing at the kitchen counter, watching TV while we ate our cereal. By then I had already read tons of stuff online about *pedes mortuus*. The Centers for Disease Control and Prevention in Atlanta had a feature page on it, and there were at least a thousand postings from people saying it wasn't new at all, that their moms had had it, or their friends, or their cats. I'd spent the night shivering in my humpy bed.

"Walking dead, eh?" said Dad. "Well, well." He never seems to be surprised.

"I know the guy. He's in my class. He's the one I don't like."

Dad nodded. I ate some Froot Loops, normally my favourite cereal. They tasted like ash. "So what should I do today?"

I meant what should I do about Imre but Dad didn't understand me.

"What do you mean? It's a weekday in September. You go to school, that's what you do. You go to school. I go to work. You face bullies and teachers, I face the Cinnaglom gum account. When you get back this evening you have homework to deal with. I have your mom. That's life. That's how it goes. The days get shorter. The leaves turn colour. Before you know it the snow is falling and the old year turns into the new one. That's the system, son. Can't fight the system."

The news was over now and the weather-lady Dad hates was winking at us. He switched her off, shrugged into his fuzzy jacket, and threw his satchel over his shoulder. The screen door banged behind him. A moment later I heard his car start.

Maybe he's never surprised because a part of him is never really here.

Buz talked about Imre in a special assembly the next morning. Imre wasn't at school, and neither were a few others from our class. The rest of us trooped into the gym first thing, and Swarty played "O Canada" on the electric keyboard, and then Buz stood by himself onstage and talked. He said that the news about Imre was true.

"I wish I could have told you all about him right away, but I was not allowed to. Now that the world knows Imre's secret, I can fill you in. He is the sole survivor of the radiation leak in Fort Sterling last year."

Buz nodded at the gasps and mutters throughout the gym.

"That's right. You remember the news stories, the investigation, the national day of mourning. The town was wiped out, including Imre's parents, but he survived. Now, after months of quarantine, the army is helping him back to normal life, and Dresden is the place they picked. We have a chance to be part of history, boys and girls. Imre Lazar is Ontario's first undead student. His body is not the same as yours. He is different. It's up to us to accept his difference, to open our arms and hearts to Imre, to welcome him into our school community. This should be easy now that we have had a chance to get to know him a little bit. It's only a surface difference, after all, like being tall or short, having straight or curly hair, light or dark skin."

I heard a lot of whispers jumbled together.

"There was a news helicopter—"

"Did you see—"

"The Fort Sterling wreath—"

"Over the town hall—"

"Undead!"

I cannot tell you how upset I was. More than upset. Upset is when you spill juice on yourself. I was horrified and aghast, muddled and pulverized, disconnected from the world, gored and tossed over the fence of sanity by the charging bull of fear. The guy who sat next to me in class, less than an arm's length away, was a—

"Zombie!"

Calvin Sponagle said it loud enough to ring through the gym. "You know what *undead* means," said Calvin. "Vampires and zombies and werewolves and like that. Imre's a zombie. What's a zombie doing at our school?"

There were murmurs of agreement around the gym. I found my own head nodding. What was Imre doing here?

"Easy, Calvin," said Buz from the stage. "Let's not be using bad words."

"You mean zom—"

"Quiet! We all know the *Z* word," said Buz, frowning down at us. "We hear it a lot, a common vulgar term for the undead. But it's an unkind word, and I do not want to hear anyone using it."

Buz was a pretty cool guy. He used to be a pro quarterback, and he could still throw a football from one end of the field to the other. When he looked stern, you did what he wanted, fast. But he was also super-nice. He went to the kindergarten classroom all the time to read stories to the little kids.

"Words can hurt," he said. "If you have ever been called a bad word, you know that. Imre is nothing like the cliché you see in movies and video games. His condition is not dangerous or contagious. He is not part of an apocalypse. He wants what you want—to make friends, to learn, to have fun. He's a child like any of you. Except that his heart isn't beating."

Swarty played a Beatles song as we shuffled out of the gym and down the hall to class. Evil-O was ahead of me. I wanted to run up to her and say, *Told you so! I knew there was something off with Imre.* But she wouldn't meet my eye. And anyway, I was too upset to enjoy being right. I had my hand on my wrist, taking my pulse. So far as I could count, my heart was beating 280 times a minute. Which was 280 times more than Imre's.

CHAPTER 6

What? You're shaking your head, right? You're thinking I should feel sorry for little orphan Imre and get over myself and try to be friends? Really? Like he's a kid with special needs—a leg brace or a hearing aid or something? Come on. You aren't going to win the high-jump competition in a leg brace, but you're not a freak. You're totally normal. (I mean, I'm not going to win the high jump either.) Imre was *dangerous*.

I admit, he'd been in class for a couple of weeks and not taken a single bite out of anyone. But who knew what would happen tomorrow, or the day after? Zombies are like hornets—you can't trust them. One sweat-drippy heat-wave morning a few summers ago there was a hornet buzzing around our front porch, and Mom told me that if I left it alone it would leave me alone, so I edged outside, being really careful to leave plenty of space between me and the hornet—and it zoomed right over and stung me anyway. Don't ask where.

I had a Fruit Roll-Up in my back pocket and the hornet must have smelled it. That part of me swelled up like a beach ball and I could not sit down for days. Evil-O laughed like a maniac every time she saw me. I feel the same way about zombies as I do about hornets. There's a level in Questcon where they come bubbling out of the floor after you with their faces eaten away and their arms falling off, and the first time I got there I screamed and dropped the controller.

Funny that memory should come up, considering what happened later.

CHAPTER 7

That night I was in the basement watching funny videos on the computer to cheer myself up when my parents got back from the emergency PTA meeting at Mrs. Berdit's. My mom called me upstairs and grabbed me by the shoulders.

"Bobby!" she said. "Tell me about the undead boy from Fort Sterling! What a tragedy to have everyone in your life dead!"

"He's sort of dead too," said Dad. "That's the point, isn't it?"

Mom ignored him.

"Mr. Buzminski was at the PTA meeting and told us the whole story," she said. "I was in tears. That poor little boy! What will happen now that everyone knows? No one is going to keep that awful Mary Lee Berdit quiet. Oh, I do not like her! She's so narrow! So hateful! I'm so angry I could spit! And so is your father!"

"Well," said Dad.

The PTA meeting had gone badly. Mrs. Berdit kept shouting that Imre didn't belong in her daughter's school, that it was a disgrace and a betrayal of trust and that she was going to do something about it. Buz said people should keep an open mind, to remember that nothing was more important than the education of our children, and that Imre was going to return to school any day now. Then Mrs. Berdit asked him to leave her house, and the meeting was over.

"Disgusting!" said Mom. "I hate that woman. I'm going to send an email of support to the school board right now."

I opened my mouth. Maybe I shouldn't have.

"Imre *is* kind of creepy," I said.

"Imre, that's right, that's his name," said Mom, making a note. "And the army is looking after him because his parents are dead. I wonder if there's anything we can do to help."

"What? He doesn't need help. A giant piano smashed into him and broke in half. Imre was fine. Mom, he's a zombie. He doesn't need any—"

"Oh, Bobby!"

"What?"

"Bobby!"

You know the tone your mom gets when you promised and promised and promised to tidy your room and you still haven't done it and now the world is falling apart and it's *your* fault? That's how she sounded.

"That word, Bobby. I don't want you using it. Mr. Buzminski has banned the word inside the school and I think he has a good point. I don't want the word used here either."

"But he is a . . . I mean, I . . ."

She stared at me with those big caring eyes. I ran upstairs. What a day. My best friend was mad at me and my mom was hurt and my desk at school was next to a *Z* word. I needed a snack. Fortunately, I kept an emergency stash of peanut butter cups in my closet.

Junk food, I thought. It doesn't let you down.

CHAPTER 8

If you Google *zombie sightings* you get twenty million results. No surprise that a national story featuring a zombie kid got noticed. My town, my school, my classmates were instant news. I don't read the paper except for the comics, but it's hard to miss headlines or front-page pictures. Trucks from CBC and CTV and CNN and a bunch of letters I didn't know crawled around the streets of Dresden. Imre's name leaked out. I saw his picture a lot. Usually he was next to a grumpy-looking guy in an army uniform.

I ran into Gezink on my way to school a few days later. The sun was in my eyes, the breeze was pushing my hair around, and I was kicking stones. Gezink had tape on his glasses. He was always breaking them. He went through about six pairs a year.

"You're alone again," he said. "You and Evil-O used to walk to school together."

"We're still friends."

Gezink pushed his glasses up his nose.

"I bet she's already there," he said. "I bet she's excited. The zombie kid is coming back to school today."

"Yeah, I saw that."

"Evil-O likes him, eh?"

"Who, Imre? A bit."

"Oh, I bet she likes him a lot."

"Shut up, Gezink."

There was a bigger crowd than usual at the school gates and along the fence. Dozens and dozens of parents and grandparents carrying signs and marching up and down. You know—protesting. They had heard that Imre was coming back too. I could read the signs from down the block. SAVE OUR SCHOOLS. SAVE OUR KIDS. A couple said NO ZOMBIES.

Four police cars sat in front of the school with their lights flashing. Yesterday there were only two. Other cars were slowing down to look, and the cops were waving them on. Horns were honking. A crowd across the street was sipping coffee and shaking their heads. A tall woman with freckles and grey hair was standing on the hood of a car, snapping pictures.

News vans were parked all over the place like yesterday, but there was more going on today. More excitement. People with suits and amazing hair were talking into microphones and pointing. Guys with TV cameras on their shoulders wandered around filming the street and school from different angles. They filmed the protesters too. They even filmed Gezink and me and Monty the crossing guard.

Something was going to happen.

Susan Berdit and her mom were at the front of the crowd, handing out protest signs. Gezink and I slid by and onto the playground, where kids were jumping around because cool stuff was going on.

When Imre's bus came down the street, it was surrounded by protesters. All the cameras turned at once. The police cleared space in front of the bus doors. Everyone was quiet, and then Imre got out. Alone.

It was the first time I'd seen him in days. He looked the same as usual but now that I knew what he was, his usual looked even weirder than before. When you know something, it's hard to go back to not knowing. Remember when you found out about Santa? Right.

And then the booing started. Susan Berdit and her mom, Mary Lee, stood in front of the crowd, pointing at the bus and booing. Susan's sign said NO ZOMBIES. She shook it up and down. The rest of the crowd took up the booing. Someone called out, "Zombie, go home!" Other people took up the cry. The word we weren't supposed to use was all over the place.

"Zombie, zombie."

Imre didn't seem to mind. He nodded glumly, like this was what he had expected.

Booing can't be good for you. You look all frown-y and eyebrow-y and your lips are pushed way out. I stared at people I'd known all my life: Susan and Dakota and Andrew and their moms and dads. Mrs. Jaconelli and Mrs. Massey from down the street. Michaela's grandma. All booing. All looking stupid.

I felt a lot of things. You know? I've never liked Susan but I was kind of hoping she and her mom would find a way to get rid of Imre. And I was still scared of Imre.

"Zombie, zombie!"

Evil-O pushed her way through the crowd, her jaw clenched and her eyes bright with anger. She held her skateboard in front of her and used it to bump past people.

"Watch where you're going, young lady!" said a grandpa with a sign.

"Oh, I was watching," she said.

She went right up to Imre. She was the only one. The booing got louder.

"Zombie lover!" shouted Susan's mom.

Evil-O's head came up. She said something to Imre, and he shrugged, and she put her arm around his shoulder.

Ew.

"Zombie lover!"

Calvin took up the cry. He was a bit ahead of me. He had his hands cupped around his mouth. His voice rang like a fire alarm.

What do you do when your best friend is making a mistake and getting booed for it? She's wrong but she's still your friend. Man, I did not like to see Evil-O with her arm around Imre. Zombie lover? I wasn't jealous—I was upset.

All right, maybe a little jealous.

Gezink was beside me. "Ow! Hold this, Bob."

He handed me something. "I hate splinters," he said.

"Uh-huh."

I was staring at Evil-O. With all these feelings sloshing around inside me, I was ready to explode. That's my only explanation for hitting Calvin over the head with the thing Gezink had given me, which turned out to be one of Susan's mom's protest signs. I didn't know what I was holding, I just stepped forward and hit Calvin with it. *Boom!* Like that. The sign was cardboard so it didn't hurt him much but he was so surprised he went down like a bowling pin. Cameras *whirred* and *clicked* and flashed.

"Who did that?" Calvin yelled. He was sitting on the ground, shaking his head. "Who did that?"

Evil-O was steering Imre towards the school and had her back to us. She turned when she heard Calvin yelling, and there I was looking like a stuffed olive, holding my sign that said ZOMBIE GO HOME.

Evil-O gave me a look I'll never forget. Mad, shocked, sad—that was bad. Betrayed—that was worse. I wanted to run right over and tell her it wasn't my sign, that I had hit Calvin because he had been booing her. I wanted to tell her I was her friend even though she had her arm around a zombie, that I would always be there for her, that I would . . . you know. But before I could do anything, the bell rang and kids started lining up.

CHAPTER 9

Evil-O comes to my place for dinner on Thursdays. Her mom works late at the shoe store and it's an understood thing. (Her dad lives in Boston, if you're wondering. She stays with him in the summer for a couple of weeks. She looks forward to going, and then seems a little sad when she comes back, like the visit wasn't quite what she thought it would be.) This Thursday was different because Evil-O wouldn't talk to me. She'd ignored me all day, even after I'd tried to explain about the sign. She walked home by herself, breezing through my front door ten minutes after me and going straight to the kitchen where Dad was shaking spices into a pot. "Hey, Mr. F.," she said.

And he said, "Hey, Evil-O, what's happening?" His glasses were steamed up. He stood away from the stove and took a sip from his glass of wine.

"Hi Evil-O," I said.

I was sitting at the kitchen table but she didn't turn

around. I might have been a potted plant for all the attention she gave me.

"Do you know much about racism, Mr. F.?"

"Not really. Why?"

"It's Imre—the new kid."

"The undead guy."

"He came back to school today and it got ugly. I just don't know how to deal with all the racists in our class, Mr. F."

"Hey!" I said.

Evil-O finally turned her head. "Racists," she said again, glaring at me.

"Oh dear," said Dad.

"Did you have racists back when you were in school, Mr. F.?"

Dad stirred, tasted, turned down the heat.

"I don't remember much racism," he said. "There were guys who said 'killer' a lot. 'Hey, killer, how's it going?' I hated those guys. And jocks and bullies and nerds. There were hot girls and whiny girls and girls with annoying laughs." He took a sip of wine. "Oh, and there was Zorka. She had an eye patch and kissed everyone."

"Ew," I said. Evil-O said it too.

"But there weren't a lot of racists. At least not in the open. One of my best friends was named Uday. He and his brother were the only Indians in the school. They must have felt like they stood out. I thought of Uday as the Indian guy the same way I thought of Townsend as the tall guy. He could dunk the basketball in grade eight. He stood out even more than Uday. Did I treat Uday any different from my other friends? Maybe. I didn't mean to. Zorka sure didn't."

"Ew," we said again.

Mom came in looking like she was about to declare war. She told me and Evil-O to go downstairs and play while she talked to Dad. He took a gulp of wine and said, "Uh-oh."

Our basement is not finished. In fact Mom says it's not even begun, but there's a couch and a TV and a computer and you can have a pretty good time. "So what do you want to do?" I asked.

Evil-O didn't say anything.

"Want to play Questcon? Sword of Honour? Or we can check YouTube. What do you want to do?"

No response. She flopped on the couch and stared up at the pipes and thingies hanging from the ceiling.

"I'm not a racist," I said. "I don't like you hanging out with Imre, that's all. He's dangerous."

She made a *ppphhh* sound.

"Look, Evil-O, you can't go on pretending not to notice me. You did it all day in school, but you can't do it now. This is my basement. That's my couch you are sitting on. We'll be eating my dad's spaghetti for dinner."

"So?" she said.

I wondered about the right way to explain how I felt.

"Here's the thing about Imre," I said. "It's not race. It's more than that. He's just—he's not—"

"Yeah?"

"He's just not human."

I guess that was the wrong way to put it because suddenly we were fighting. She jumped on me. I squirmed away and got to my feet but she knocked me down again. We wrestled around on the cold basement floor, but the fight didn't last long because—well, because she's stronger than me. She got in another punch and another and I started to wheeze. I do that when I get hit in the chest. What can I say? I'm delicate. Dr. Sophie says I have something called false asthma. It feels like asthma but it isn't really.

I made a *hehhhhhh* sound, trying to inhale.

"You're stupid, Bob. Imre is all alone in a strange place. You have no idea what he's going through. He doesn't even have foster parents. Those two who look after him are army doctors. He needs help, not boos from scared pathetic racists like you."

Dinner was a strange meal, with me wheezing and Evil-O not looking at me and Mom checking the TV every few minutes. The spaghetti was good.

He needs help. That's Evil-O. If I had a dollar for every broken bird or stray cat she's brought home and taken care of, I'd be rich. There's an old guy who plays the flute around town, leaving a hat on the sidewalk for spare change. Same clothes, winter and summer. Same creaky tunes on the flute. I walk by without looking. But every time she passes—every single time—Evil-O gives him some change.

Halfway through dessert Mom went to the den where the big TV is. I heard her swearing, which she doesn't do very much. We all went to the den, and there was our school.

44

It said so underneath: WESTWOOD ELEMENTARY SCHOOL, DRESDEN, ONTARIO. This was only the hundredth time I had seen it on the news but it was still kind of weird. There were the signs and the school bus and the people booing.

"Zibby Stinson saw this segment online and called me at work," said Mom. "It's the lead story, would you believe it?"

There was a close-up of Imre getting off the bus.

"Is that him?" Mom asked us. "Is that the poor boy all the fuss is about? We've talked and talked about him but I've never seen him."

Poor boy? I thought.

"That's him," said Evil-O.

And there *she* was on TV, walking up to Imre. This was even weirder than seeing my school—watching my best friend on TV. When she put her arm around Imre's shoulders, I could feel my spaghetti dinner sloshing around in my stomach.

Now Susan's mom was talking to a newswoman. The situation was intolerable, said Mrs. Berdit. Imre was dangerous and different.

"Let him be with his own kind!" she said.

The newswoman pointed out that Imre was the only survivor of the Fort Sterling nuclear accident. "He is the only one of his kind," she said.

"I don't care!" said Susan's mom. "He shouldn't be in my daughter's class! He's a monster! Save our schools!" she shouted, and she shook her fist at the camera. Under her picture was the phrase MARY LEE BERDIT, CONCERNED PARENT.

45

Dad laughed. Mom told him to shush and he said he couldn't help it, that Mary Lee was funny. Mom said no, she was dangerous. Dad said *umph*.

"Imre's not a monster!" said Evil-O.

"Of course he's not!" said Mom. "Evil-O, you did a wonderful thing, standing up to all those angry people. I'm proud of you. And I—*OHHHhhhhhhhh*."

She gasped, her voice trailing off, getting softer and sadder and deeper.

CHAPTER 10

It wasn't weird to see myself on TV, like it was to see Evil-O. I felt like I was watching a stranger, a chunky kid in too-tight pants who stepped forward and clubbed Calvin over the head with his sign. The camera guys must have had a long lens because the details were sharp. I could see the rip in the back pocket of my backpack.

"Bobby!" whispered Mom. "Bobby, that's you."

There's a time to lie, but not when they have film footage.

The news segment was over now and they were showing a commercial about fertilizer. Apparently, it was a good thing to put on your lawn at this time of year. The lawn on TV was sighing happily.

Mom wasn't.

"My own son!" she said. "Bobby, Bobby, how could you? We've always taught you to accept other people's differences!"

"But—"

"And violence, Bobby. Violence is no solution. We have tried to teach you that too. Haven't you been listening? Carrying the sign is bad enough. But using it as a weapon. Aren't you ashamed of yourself, Bobby!"

She gave an impressively long sigh. I didn't know she could hold in that much air. It went on and on and on.

The whole situation was so unfair. She was upset with me for carrying a protest sign, and also for attacking Calvin. Did she think Calvin was on Imre's side? I opened my mouth to explain, but what came out wasn't an explanation. I got mad.

"No, I'm not ashamed of myself!" I said. "I feel fine. I thought there was something weird about Imre, and it turns out I was right. There *is* something weird about him. He's undead. That is very weird, no matter what you all say."

I turned to Dad, standing next to me. "You want to yell at me too?" I said. "You want to be disappointed in me because I tell the truth? I'll say it again: Imre is weird. I don't like Susan or her mom but they're right about him!"

I stomped off to the kitchen, looked at my pudding but decided I couldn't eat it, and headed upstairs.

It's hard to feel anything else when you're mad. Mad takes up a lot of space inside you. I didn't even have room for dessert.

ad cleared my cereal bowl and—surprise—put it in the dishwasher. He usually drifts away after breakfast and lets me take care of my own stuff. I asked if Mom was at work or still home and he rolled his eyes.

"You'll find out soon enough."

What did he mean?

"I guess she's still upset with me, huh?"

"A little. Don't worry too much. She'll get over it. So will Evil-O."

I doubted that. Evil-O would get over it when I changed my mind about Imre—or when he bit me and I became a zombie. Not before.

"Your mom loves you, son. But she cares about other things like justice and equality too. You've heard her story about going to jail back when she was in college—maybe more than once."

"Maybe more than a hundred times."

49

Dad ghosted a smile at me. He must have heard it, like, a thousand times.

There were more protesters and more TV cameras in front of the school today. The protesters stood in a semicircle facing Susan's mom, like a choir. Mrs. Berdit would wave her hands and shout, "One, two, three, four," and the others would shout, "Kick the zombie out the door." They did that a couple times, then someone shouted, "Zombie, go home!" and that caught on. They shouted it over and over. It was spirited and kind of boring at the same time, like a parade.

Buz and an important-looking woman stood over by the gate with reporters clustered around them, pointing microphones and shouting questions. The woman did the talking. Her teeth showed white against her skin. The police added to the entertainment value. Three cars' worth today, with their lights flashing and radios hissing. Neighbourhood people stood across the road with cups of coffee, taking it all in. Mrs. Jenkin, who has lived at the corner as long as I can remember, was in a chair on her front lawn.

That's when I heard the honking.

Three minivans rolled slowly up Westwood with their horns going. They parked around the corner from the school and a dozen people got out, looking grim and determined, holding signs. I was close enough to read a couple of them. One sign said JUSTICE. Another said UNDEAD RIGHTS.

What on earth?

The TV guys liked this new development. They headed over for close-ups, crouching to shoot, cameras steady on their shoulders. The reporters left Buz and the important woman. They shouted questions, pointed microphones, blocked traffic all the way up the hill.

The group from the minivans marched up the sidewalk towards the school in a clump, waving their signs. My stomach turned over.

I recognized most of the new protesters. Mr. and Mrs. Jin, who run the pharmacy, Travis's mom, Doug, who owns the No Frills grocery store and gets his picture in the paper all the time, Mom's friend Mrs. Stinson, who writes poetry and teaches swimming at the YMCA, and, yes, Mom herself.

Oh pork chops! (I heard an old guy say that once, when he stepped in a puddle. He shook the water off his shoe and said it like it was a swear word. *Pork chops!* It stuck with me.) Mom had a big flowery shirt on, and her old blue jeans with the ripped knees that she can't do up without sucking in her stomach. Her sign said WE LOVE YOU, IMRE.

You'll find out soon enough, Dad had said.

Mom swayed from side to side as she sang. I recognized the tune—she had sung it to me when I was a little kid. The two groups of protesters faced off against each other at the school gate. It was a bit like the start of a football play when the two teams line up. The police got ready to referee. The singing got louder and so did the chanting. Deep in their hearts, Mom's protesters believed that they would overcome someday. Susan's mom's group wanted the zombies to go home.

The cameras were busy. When Imre's bus came over the hill, Mom linked arms with Mrs. Stinson and the two of them cheered. Mom's face shone like Christmas morning. I couldn't look at her and I couldn't look away.

A gull floated above the bus, staying totally still, using the wind to keep itself in the same place.

Imre climbed down to boos and cheers. Reporters lined up along the school fence, shouting questions at him. I heard bits and pieces.

"What's it like . . ."

"How do you feel . . ."

"Do you wish . . ."

"What do you want . . ."

Imre looked the way he usually did, kind of glum. The important lady stepped forward. Was it my imagination or did she hesitate before shaking hands? She had to bend way down to do it—she was a tall one. I did notice her wipe her hand on a tissue afterwards.

Music—a drum and synthesizer riff—boomed across the playground. I don't know how to write it out. *Chicka chicka clam diddy,* or something. The riff repeated, and repeated again, and I heard a woman shouting on top of it.

The challenge of living,
And habit of giving,
And the need for forgiving,
Living with the unliving.

It was Mrs. Stinson, freestyling.

The living are leaving,
Unjust are deceiving
And plots they are weaving
While Justice is grieving
For lack of believing.
(Chicka chicka clam diddy boom.)

The important lady had her mouth open wide enough to swallow a peach. The gull was gone.

The new boy is Imre
His parents named him, they
Died in a grim way
Seem like yesterday
To Imre.

I put my fingers in my ears and turned to run. And there was the weird pumpkin face again—round and toothy, peering for just a second out of a window near the front of the bus. Then disappearing. I grabbed the kid standing next to me. It was Andrew's little brother, Leo. Grade four.

"You see that face? In the bus window?" I asked him.

He shook his head. He was probably scared to talk to a seventh grader.

"Well it was there," I said.

"Sure it was," he said. "You're Bob Fuller, aren't you? You're in my brother's class. He says you're an oddball. You probably made up the face in the window."

Maybe he wasn't scared of me.

The bell rang and we headed for the doors. The protesters stopped chanting and singing. The TV people started packing up. The neighbours went inside now that the entertainment was over. I made the mistake of catching Mom's eye. She waved her sign.

"Yoo-hoo, Bobby!" she yelled across the playground.

She looked happy and *fulfilled*, you know? She'd done a good deed and wasn't mad at me anymore. And she was bursting to tell me.

"I love you, Bobby!"

Her words echoed. She waved vigorously. There weren't many kids left outside, but they all turned around. Andrew's brother was laughing at me. He laughed and laughed. When did little kids get tough?

Aw, pork chops.

CHAPTER 12

Things got worse. Things can always get worse. I was leaning against the portable, crunching gently, when Calvin Sponagle grabbed my collar from behind. I shook myself free and ran, scattering Cheezies like confetti. Around the portable and out into the field with my heart pounding inside and Calvin pounding behind. He caught me after the shortest of sprints, dragged me to the grass alley on the shady side of the school where no one ever goes, and pushed me to the ground.

"It was you, Bob," he said. "You're the one who hit me yesterday. It was on TV. I saw it. My dad saw it. He was so mad he broke a table with a baseball bat."

The ground was soft and muddy on this side of the school. My knees were getting wet.

"Sorry," I said. "But you were booing Evil-O. She's my friend."

"She's as weird as you are. She likes that zombie."

Something deep inside me went *ouch*. "Do you really

think so, Calvin?" I said. "Do you think she *likes* Imre? I mean like, *likes* him?"

I tried to get up but Calvin pushed me down again. He's been pushing people around the playground for years. He probably didn't start life as a bully but he sure was one now. The real thing. Angry and mean, with little piggy eyes and enormous muscles. He even smelled awful, like mud. No, wait, that was me.

"You like him too, don't you, Bob. You sit with him."

"Who, Imre? Because as a matter of fact—"

"Zombie lover!"

"I was carrying a sign," I said, thinking quickly. "It said ZOMBIE GO HOME. Would I carry a sign telling him to go home if I was his friend?"

But that only reminded Calvin.

"You hit me with the sign. My dad was mad."

And he pushed me so hard I had to sit down, and then he stomped away.

"My mom is not going to be happy with these muddy pants," I yelled after him. "I'm going to get in trouble. Just letting you know."

When you think of zombies, you don't think smart, and Imre sure wasn't. It didn't seem to bother him though. "Well, well," he would say. "Another test, another failure. At least I have my good looks." And he'd make a creaky sound that was his way of laughing. Or we'd be doing silent reading and he'd ask about the *M* word at the top of the page. "Mysterious,"

Ms. Eiger would say, or "Mustard," or whatever the word was. "Ah, that's what it looks like," he'd say. And a minute later he'd apologize and ask about the same word again. "You have to remember I'm a zombie. My brain is weak. There's no blood getting up there."

Yeah, he called himself a zombie. He got away with it, but none of us could.

Evil-O made me change seats with her so she was sitting next to Imre. She would go over things with him, patient as rust, sounding words out syllable by syllable. I'd turn around and see them with their heads together. She was better friends with him now than ever.

Know what else? I didn't like sitting in front of Imre. If I was going to be within arm's length of a zombie, I wanted to be able to see him coming.

Ms. Eiger handed out a flyer at the end of the day. Usually flyers are about bake sales and book drives and class trips. This one wasn't.

EDUCATING IMRE: OUR NEW NEIGHBOUR
Living and Undead Together!
Make your voice heard! Come to the Town Hall meeting.
Dresden Town Hall
Thursday, September 26
6:00 p.m.
With Superintendent Nelson, Board of Education

On the flyer there was a shot of Imre standing beside Buz and the important lady from this morning. Farther down were more pictures of Imre: getting on his school bus, on a swing somewhere, and walking beside a stream with a woman and the grumpy-looking man I had seen him with in other pictures.

Imre moaned. "Dr. Bernstein is not going to be happy."

He shook his head and all this dark flaky stuff fell out of his hair. Some of it drifted towards my desk. I shuddered and got out the hand sanitizer.

I was dragging my backpack out of my locker when I heard the whisper:

"Zombie lovers."

I straightened up and looked around. Evil-O's locker is near mine. She'd heard the whisper too.

"Who said that?" she demanded. "Susan? Calvin?"

They were walking together. Which was odd because they have always hated each other. Susan lives in a mansion on Tremayne, the fanciest street in town, with an indoor swimming pool. Calvin's on King Street, over Jim's Pizza, living with his awful dad and big brother and a bunch of guns and footballs and televisions—at least I guess that's what's there because that's all Calvin talks about. But here he was with Susan, the two of them walking side by side down the hall.

"Racists!" hissed Evil-O. *Racists* is a good word for hissing. She slammed her locker and took off without a backwards look at them or me, which hurt in a new kind of way. Evil-O was ignoring me. I wasn't even worth getting mad at anymore. I was both a racist and a zombie lover, and I had no friends.

Dresden is flat, but I walked home feeling like every step was uphill.

CHAPTER 13

We ate dinner in front of the TV so Mom could watch the news. Dad said he would record it so we could watch it later and Mom asked if he remembered trying to record the documentary on jazz and getting wrestling instead. Dad said *umph* and brought plates and napkins into the TV room.

The news always starts in a faraway place where the clothes are different and it's a historic day for there—wherever it is. Today it was guys wearing those head scarves, sitting at a table with a piece of paper. Dull? You'd better believe it. I thought they'd never finish signing their names. Ham for dinner, and beans, and potatoes with a chewy cheesy sauce. Pretty good. Actually, the potatoes were better than pretty good. I save the best stuff to the end and that's usually the meat, but today it was the potatoes. Next on the news was the prime minister making a speech. Also dull. I wondered how the prime minister would look in a head scarf. Or the news guy, whose hair sat on the top of his head like a hamburger bun. He shuffled his papers.

"Now we bring you a special feature on the elementary school in Ontario where opinions are sharply divided . . ."

Mom went, "Shhhhhh," even though no one was talking.

There was a lot of footage. Imre looked glum. Buz looked grim. Dakota's mom booed and looked stupid. Mrs. Stinson rhymed *freedom* and *be done* and snapped her fingers right into the camera. There was a shot of Mom in her flowered shirt and a close-up of her sign saying that she loved Imre. Then it was back to hamburger-head and a panel of experts on something—not zombies.

And then the phone began to ring.

And ring.

I kept thinking it might be Evil-O but it wasn't, not once. A protest friend of Mom's, the local newspaper, another protester, a magazine reporter, a telemarketer. Mom said, "Did you see?" And, "What a key issue this is!" And, "Wasn't that great?" And, "Of course I have a few minutes." And, "No thank you."

My plate was empty, the taste of potatoes a faint memory, like last year's birthday party. I went up to my room. I could see the Foubert house across the street. Their van pulled in and the girls raced each other up the walk. The street lights came on as I watched. A small dark shape swizzled and darted around the front of our house. A bat. The hairs on my arm tingled and my heart picked up speed. I thought about going for a walk, but I hadn't seen Razor in a few days and I didn't want to take a chance on meeting him.

CHAPTER 14

Imre and I were down in the basement with the lights low. We played hockey for a while, on our knees with little plastic sticks and a Ping-Pong ball for a puck. Imre was a lousy goalie but a good sport and he laughed his creaky laugh as he let in shot after shot. Then we were playing the castle level of AdventureQuest and I wanted to shoot him but the trigger on my controller was gone. A new player came into the castle and shot me, and I looked away from the TV and there was Evil-O sitting on the couch next to Imre. She stuck her tongue out at me and grabbed Imre's hand. My heart fell, *plop*, like snow from the roof. He lunged forward with his mouth open wide enough for me to see the gaps between his blackened teeth. Was he going to bite Evil-O or kiss her? The lights flickered and went out. I heard a scream.

"Bobby? Are you okay?" Mom stood in my doorway.

"Yeah."

"Bad dream?"

I wiped my face with my pyjama sleeve.

"Yeah."

"Want to talk about it?"

"No."

CHAPTER 15

Ms. Eiger was slow. She didn't walk, she *eroded* across the room. And the way she talked! Listening to her explain fractions or the . . . Iroquois was . . . enough to drive you . . . . crazy. The morning flowed like cement until she wrote the words CLASS ELECTIONS on the blackboard, and DAYS LEFT and the number 5. "That's how many . . . days before you vote for class . . . president," she told us. "Now I'd like you to . . . think about some . . ." She took a deep breath. We waited.

"I nominate Susan," said Dakota.

". . . candidates," Ms. Eiger finished.

"Susan," said Dakota again. "Why don't we just vote for her now. It'll save time."

Debbie, sitting behind her, nodded vigorously. I saw Susan in profile and could tell she was trying hard not to smile.

Evil-O growled. Susan was class president last year and the year before and Evil-O hates every single thing about her.

Not just the way she dresses or talks or tries to take charge of things, or her friends or fancy lunches or pool parties. Everything. "I hate the way she breathes," she told me once.

"We want to have at . . . least two candidates," said Ms. Eiger, writing SUSAN BERDIT on the board.

"Yay, Susan!" said Debbie.

Evil-O's shoulders were tensing up. I wanted to show her that I still liked her, even if she was ignoring me. One way would be to suggest her for class president. But before I could put my hand up I heard Imre's voice.

"I nominate Evil-O," he said.

The whole class turned to stare. Imre put up his hands.

"I know, I know." His voice was oddly deep for someone so small. "Who would want *my* support? I'm hurting Evil-O's chances. She probably wishes I had not spoken. Still, there it is. She is my friend and I nominate her."

Ms. Eiger was frowning like she usually did when she heard Imre's voice. I wondered if she knew she was doing it. She wrote Evil-O's name on the board slowly. Debbie was whispering to Dakota. Gezink was looking at Susan and then at Imre, back and forth, like he was watching a tennis game.

Evil-O whispered her thanks to Imre. "I won't win," she said. "But I can't let Susan get in without us having to vote. You're the best, Imre."

His nails were cracked. He had a piece of tape on one wrist, like a bandage. Just looking at him made me shudder.

###

66

Today was spelling and Imre didn't get any of the rules. Ms. Eiger tried to explain *i* before *e* and he kept shaking his head. She . . . spoke . . . slowly, and he understood even slower than that. I thought I was going to become an old man before they were done. I think that was the first time sitting near Imre was boring. Boredom isn't fun, but it's better than fear. Fear is a hurt, a physical pain sharp as a slap or a needle. Bored is like being full of cheese.

Speaking of pain, Calvin caught me again at afternoon recess. Gezink and I were shooting hoops and Calvin stepped out of nowhere to grab a long rebound.

"I'll play too," he said.

When I looked over, Gezink was gone. Typical Gezink. The court was on the far side of the school, away from the street. No teacher nearby. No news helicopter overhead.

"Guess it's just you and me, zombie lover," said Calvin.

I took a step back.

"I'd *like* to play with you," I said. "It'd be great. Really, Calvin, you and I don't spend enough time together. But gosh, wouldn't you know it, recess is moving along and I have this, uh, this, uh, *thing* I should be—"

Calvin surprised me by throwing the ball at my head. Next thing I knew I was on my back on the pavement with him bending over me.

"I should tell you that I have something wrong with my heart," I said. "Endo-something. It's a dangerous condition. My, uh, chest could explode at any moment."

I was lying on dark grey asphalt with a curved white line. Top of the key. I was sort of leaning back on my elbows. He put his foot on my stomach to hold me down. Embarrassing.

"You know, my doctor says that the middle of the day is the most vulnerable time for us endo sufferers. If my heart explodes now, you'll get in real trouble. You don't want that, do you?"

I panted a little and tried for a smile that would be winning and kind of pathetic at the same time. I don't think I pulled it off.

"Hey Sponagle! Leave the poor kid alone."

Evil-O and Imre were walking across the empty basketball court. I did not like them being together. I especially didn't like the idea of being saved by them. My embarrassment rate went up. If I was, say, at a five out of ten on the embarrassment scale before, I was now at least at a seven.

"Poor kid?" I said. "Who, me?" I tried to roll out from under Calvin's shoe. He didn't let me. "I'm not a poor kid. I'm totally comfortable. Calvin and I were just, uh, playing. Weren't we, Calvin?"

"No we weren't," said Calvin.

CHAPTER 16

"Go away, Sponagle," said Evil-O. "Leave Bob alone!"

"Yes," said Imre. "Please leave Bob alone."

Calvin took his foot off me and went over to Imre. His hands were fists.

"Leave Bob alone—or what? You going to smash me, zombie boy? I am not a piano." Which is not a phrase you hear very often. And then, without any warning, he bent down and punched Imre in the chest.

"Hey!" I said.

The guy had taken a punch because of me and I owed him something. Not much but something. A *hey*. I didn't move, mind you.

Evil-O jumped between the two boys and shouted at Calvin to stop.

"I'm sorry, I do not understand." Imre's voice was totally normal. You'd never know he had just been punched. "Did

69

you hit me because you don't like zombies, or is it something personal?"

"Come on, fight me!" Calvin moved away from Evil-O. He was in a UFC stance, side-on to Imre, bouncing up and down on his toes.

"Why should I fight you?"

Imre didn't get it, but I thought I did. Calvin had always been the strongest kid around, and now—maybe—he wasn't. He couldn't stand not knowing so he was challenging Imre to a kind of duel. Like in the Wild West when they had to decide who was the faster gun.

There's usually a good guy and a bad guy in a duel, but not this time. Calvin was a bully and Imre was scary. It's hard to cheer for someone if you're afraid he might start taking bites out of you.

Imre walked away. Calvin made a running jump, trying to bring him down, but he wouldn't go down and Calvin ended up wrapped around his shoulders. A kind of piggyback, only with the size difference it looked more like an elephant sitting on a fire hydrant. I couldn't help giggling.

Evil-O took a second to glare at me before yelling at the boys to stop.

Mrs. Swartman came around the corner as Imre got a hand under Calvin and tossed him into the air. Not much effort seemed to be involved—it was like he was tossing a coin. Calvin helicoptered around and landed with a *whump* on the grass. Swarty helped him to his feet and sent us all to the principal's office. Even me.

"But I didn't do anything," I said.

"You were there," Swarty said.

I thought about that as we headed into the school. If being there is enough, then you can always get in trouble, can't you? I mean, you're always somewhere.

CHAPTER 17

We waited outside Mr. Buzminski's office. Evil-O and Imre were on one bench, me and Calvin on the other. Calvin was sighing and shaking his head. I checked my pulse against the clock on the wall. Evil-O asked what I was doing.

"Nothing."

"You've got your finger on your wrist."

The secretary picked up the phone for the eighth or ninth time since we'd been there. "Yes, this is Westwood Elementary School in Dresden," she said. "No, I can't give out any student information. No, I'm afraid Mr. Buzminski is busy. Goodbye."

Buz stood us in a line while he walked back and forth in front of us and talked about not making the school look bad.

"The whole world is paying attention to us," he said. "I do not want controversy to spill out onto the playground. Let the parents protest, let the media talk all they want, but I will not have my students fighting. Is that understood, Calvin?"

Calvin's jaw hung open. He wasn't tracking too well.

Buz turned to Imre.

"You have to keep your cool, young man. You may be a victim here, but you are so strong that you could hurt someone."

His desk phone had buttons to show the outside lines. There were five of them and they were all flashing. Five people he wasn't talking to.

"And as for you, Bob and Evil-O—"

"I can't promise," Evil-O interrupted, her jaw set like concrete. "If someone's mean to Imre, I'm going to get them. Hear that, Calvin? And tell Susan Berdit as well."

Buz transferred his frown to me.

"I was just there," I said. "I'm a victim too."

The bell rang. School was over. Buz made us shake hands and shooed us out of the office. Walking down the empty hall, Calvin seemed smaller, softer. Think of a balloon when it starts to leak air. Like that. We passed a lone third-grader getting his backpack from his locker. Calvin didn't push him or trip him or anything. Just kept walking with his eyes on the floor.

I had my hand in my pocket to warm it up. Shaking hands with Imre was like reaching into the freezer.

CHAPTER 18

Imre and Evil-O were going to her place again. She was helping him with his reading. Ms. Eiger didn't want to waste class time on him, and had stopped answering his questions. *You know they're un . . . teachable,* she'd said privately to Mr. Dejardins, only Evil-O overheard and had to do something about it. I asked her why she was acting like his big sister, and she got all red-faced and didn't answer me.

So they were going to get dropped off by his school bus, and I was walking alone. No protests after school. Some of the protesters had to go to work and others were driving their kids around. Mrs. Berdit had to take Susan to piano lessons and modern dance classes and soccer practices and Toastmasters meetings and something called Opportunity Club. (I am not making any of this up. Susan's extracurricular activities were a big part of her conversation. I could get tired just hearing about her life).

The clouds were grey-white and greasy looking, like slush. I felt slushy myself.

I tried to cheer myself up by paying real attention to my neighbourhood, noticing details: Mrs. Dithyramb rocking on her front porch. Mrs. Browne's baby, Will, whose feet stuck way out in front of the stroller. A shiny new delivery truck parked in the Furillos' driveway—Mr. and Mrs. Furillo have a market on Highway 2 near the mall. Mrs. Wing-Wedderburn bent over, stretching. She ran miles every day and made my dad sigh when he drove past her. The Foubert kids playing catch on their front lawn, shrieking at each other. I was trying to remember if I had eaten all the crackers yesterday. Onion crackers and cheddar cheese would be a great snack.

I didn't think about Evil-O and Imre with their heads together, sounding out words. No, I did not.

A door slammed. The Foubert kids were gone, leaving their ball and baseball gloves on the lawn. Mrs. Dithyramb was inside. The street was suddenly deserted.

You know the way an idea arrives in your brain like a car crashing through your living room—*boom*, and there it is? I got one of those. Only it wasn't an idea. I was hurrying up my driveway when it hit me from the side, knocking me to the ground.

Razor.

Razor was a mastiff, belonged to Mrs. Good from around the corner. Black and brown, about the size and weight of a stuffed chair, but much more vicious. Razor attacked kids, cats, other dogs—whatever he could catch. People stayed inside when he went for a walk. It was no good complaining about him because Mrs. Good's brother was the chief of police. My mom called the dog a necessary evil, and told me to walk on the other side of the street. If you leave him alone, he'll leave you alone, she said. I didn't believe her.

Now he'd caught me. His front paws were on my chest. His mouth hung open, inches from my face. It was like looking into a furnace. He barked once, twice, and lunged at my neck. I screamed. His jaws closed and locked—but not on me.

As Evil-O told me later, she and Imre were in her living room, and looked up to see Razor charging after me like Fate. They ran, reaching me as the dog was in mid-lunge. Imre's arm came between the dog's mouth and my neck.

Razor bit hard and hung on. I was close enough to get dog slobber on my cheek, which would normally have me freaking out and running for soap and water and sanitizer. But this was not normally. I had more important things to freak out about. Imre, for instance. The dog's teeth practically met around his wrist. I couldn't imagine the agony he must be in. He didn't scream or cry, though, just stared at his arm and sighed.

"Maybe you should move, Bob," he said.

I scrambled out from under the dog. Imre's expression was disappointed. And now *this* is happening, he seemed to be thinking. Razor shook his heavy head back and forth, making the metal bits of the leash jingle.

Evil-O had hold of one floppy ear. I tugged at his collar. We could not pull the dog off. I wondered where Mrs. Good was.

"Better stand back," said Imre.

He was as calm as mould. He stood up and lifted his hand, higher and higher, taking no notice of the dog's weight. When his hand was well over his head and the dog was off the ground, he brought his arm down hard, bending at the waist to thump Razor onto the driveway. *Whump!*

I felt like a damsel in distress watching my champion do battle, which was not cool. But let me tell you, I would rather be rescued than ruined. Ask any damsel in distress and I'm sure she would say the same thing.

The second time Razor hit the driveway he went limp. You could see it. His jaws were still clenched but his eyes were closed and the growling stopped. Imre pulled his arm free, and the dog lay on the driveway without moving.

CHAPTER 19

What do you say to a guy you hate but who has just saved your life?

"Holy crap," I said.

Then I thought I could do better than that.

"Thanks, man. Thanks a lot."

This was the second time today. He'd already taken a punch for me.

He shrugged.

The street was quiet. It wasn't raining, but it would soon. I could smell the dampness in the air. I was panting, coming down from the shock. I rubbed dog slobber off my cheek.

Imre gestured at Razor, lying on his side on the driveway. "It was probably my fault that the dog was upset in the first place. My smell was in the air. Animals hate me. It's the undead thing."

"Well," I said, "I owe you."

"No, no."

I took a deep breath. I wanted to do something about Imre. To act, you know. I could only think of one thing.

Samantha Foubert came out of her house and stood on the front porch with a Popsicle in her hand. She stared over at us, the way little kids will stare.

"Come on, Imre," said Evil-O. "Let's go back to my place. Your bus will be along in an hour and we are only halfway through that Ding and Yo Yo book."

"Sorry!"

It came out louder than I intended. I cleared my throat and tried again. "Sorry, Imre."

He turned. "For what?"

"For, I don't know, everything."

"I don't understand, Bob. How can you be sorry for everything?"

"The way I've been acting. And thinking. About you."

"I still don't—"

"I looked at you and all I saw was a—"

I stopped. My face got hotter as the blood rushed up.

"A zombie?"

I nodded. "I didn't see a person—a real, undead person. A real person, I mean, who happens to be undead."

I felt embarrassed and stupid, and kind of like a liar too. I mean, part of me was still scared of Imre. But I just could not go on hating a guy who had saved my life twice in one day.

He showed his ragged teeth.

"It's okay, Bob. I know how you feel. If I wasn't me, I'd be scared of me too."

"Really?"

"Sometimes I catch sight of myself in the mirror and have to step back."

This made me smile, which was better than blushing. I wasn't ready to be best friends yet, and I didn't know what to think about him and Evil-O, but at least some stuff was out in the open.

Speaking of Evil-O, she let out a whoop and threw both her hands up. We high-tenned. The relief and happiness on her face made a lot of things seem brighter.

"Hey Bob," she said.

"Hey Evil-O."

Big smiles. My heart did a little shimmy.

"Come on, Imre," I said. "High-five, man!"

"What? Oh, I see. All right," he said. "No, wait."

He sighed, looking down. His right sleeve was shredded from the dog's teeth. A strip of duct tape hung loose and flapping. I remembered noticing it earlier that day. Below the tape, I saw the end of a wrist, bones and flesh and white stringy things, and . . . and that was it.

We couldn't do our high-five because he didn't have a hand.

"Oh dear," he said.

The dog was making a choking noise. Imre went down on one knee and reached into the dog's mouth with his other hand. His only hand, I should say.

Evil-O and I stared at each other.

"Are you okay?" I asked him. The ridiculousness of the question hit me, and I added, "Apart from losing your hand, I mean."

81

"I'm fine. The hand is loose. This happens all the time. It's just a nuisance."

"But aren't you ... doesn't it hurt?"

"Nothing hurts me. Remember the piano? Zombies are strong, Bob."

He was up to his forearm, fishing around in the dog's gullet. He gave a grunt of effort, pulling free and straightening up with the hand he found in there—his hand—in his other hand. All those fingers lined up together made me think of sausages.

"Now what?" said Evil-O. "Do you have to go to the hospital?"

"No, no. But if you have any tape, that'd be great."

And before I knew it, I found myself saying that I had some duct tape in a drawer and that we should all go to my place. I unlocked the front door and stood aside.

"Razor! Razor!"

Mrs. Good has a voice you could split firewood with. She came into view around the bend in our street. Drops of rain spattered on the driveway. The leaves on Evil-O's maple tree were showing their undersides. The dog lifted his head, shook himself, and got up slowly. It took him a couple of tries.

"Raaaa-zorrrrr! Here!"

The stumpy tail wagged. The dog stumbled forward. And the rain came down.

CHAPTER 20

The duct tape went around and around, forearm to wrist, with a loop of tape around the thumb. Imre couldn't do it himself so I held his hand in place while Evil-O wrapped the tape. I did *not* scream like a little girl. It was a close call, though. I mean, I was holding this piece of cold human flesh, making sure the ends of bone in the wrist lined up with the bits sticking out of Imre's arm. I could see veins and tendons and muscles and felt myself getting light-headed. I had to take some deep breaths.

Evil-O wrapped the tape neatly, smoothed it down, and cut another strip. When she was done, Imre tested his hand. He could bend it and make a fist. "How does your hand still work?" she asked. "There's just tape holding it together."

"Well, if you tape G.I. Joe's arm back on, you can still move it around, can't you? Until the tape comes off again, that is," he continued gloomily.

After all the yeck, I didn't feel like cheese and crackers

for snack. I found a box of Popsicles in the freezer and we had those instead. Imre chomped away at his Popsicle like it was a Twizzler. It was gone in five seconds. I got him another one and he ate that up too. Cherry juice all over his face. I gave him a paper towel and used one myself. There was still a bit of hand sanitizer in the bottom of the bottle.

"I don't understand about the blood," said Evil-O. She was wearing a Band-Aid where Razor had scratched her. "How do you get amputated and not bleed?"

"Oh, there's blood in there," he said. "But it's thick and hard to find. At the hospital they ended up scraping it out."

I shuddered, thinking of his veins filled with red sludge.

"And it didn't hurt?"

"I tell you, Evil-O, nothing hurts me."

"Oh, that is cool. Isn't it cool, Bob?"

"No," I said.

The phone rang. It was a woman from a magazine wanting to interview Mom. "Or anyone who knows anything about the protests at Westwood Elementary," she said.

"I go there."

"Do you?" she asked with a lot of warmth. "Do you *really*? That's *fascinating*. So Tara Fuller is your mom? That's *great*. What's *your* name?"

"Bob," I said.

"Hello there, Bob. I'm Natalie. You know about the protests, of course. And if you go to the school you must know Imre, the undead boy."

Her voice was like syrup dripping off a stack of pancakes.

"Yeah," I said.

"Wonderful. I have some questions about him. But the person I *really* want to find out about is the mystery girl. Do you know her, Bob?"

"Who?"

"The girl with the skateboard, who stands next to Imre in all the news clips. At the magazine we're calling her Imre's girlfriend."

"Who was that?" Evil-O asked as I sat back down. Our kitchen table is round. She sat between us. She was the tallest of the three of us. Imre was the shortest by a long shot.

"Wrong number," I said

Mom shook Imre's hand so hard I was afraid it would fall off again. She said, "How wonderful to meet you!" And, "We've heard so much about you!" And, "Oh you poor boy!" She said that eight or nine times. She called him a hero and an example to all of us, and took a cell phone picture with him, crouching to get her head next to his. She hugged me and said how pleased she was that my eyes were finally opened and I wasn't a racist anymore. "Look at you three now—Imre and Evil-O and Bob—best friends!"

It was pretty awful.

She invited him and Evil-O for dinner. Evil-O ran home to leave a note for her mom. Imre made a phone call from our kitchen.

Mom wanted to make his favourite dinner. She coughed a couple of times and asked if he wanted, uh, brains. She could go to the butcher shop and see if they had some, she said.

Dad was in the living room and overheard her question. He

said did that mean we had to eat brains too? Mom said that it was a good thing to try new foods. Dad said he didn't need any more brains, and Mom said, Oh yes he did, and he said, Very funny, but seriously if she planned on serving brains for dinner tonight she should say so right then, and he'd go out for pizza.

Imre told my mom that he was not a picky eater. "But thank you for asking."

We went downstairs to play Death Squads while we waited for Evil-O to get back. He was lousy. I killed him eight times in one series. He was a good loser, though.

"Dead again," he said. "That's me, all right."

It was hard to keep hating him or even being scared of him. I remembered Mrs. Swartman stopping at our table that first day, asking what was for lunch. I said lasagna.

"Cheese sandwich," said Evil-O.

"Brain sandwich," said Imre.

Swarty froze. "That's a joke, right?"

Anyone who can laugh at himself is a good guy.

Now that it was just the two of us I asked a question I'd wondered about for a while.

"Is it fun, being undead?"

"Fun?" He made it sound like a foreign word.

"Yeah. I mean, you can't die, right? Not again. So there's a whole bunch of things you don't have to worry about. Getting run over, choking, falling into a hole, drowning, being electrocuted, catching a horrible disease, having a heart attack, having your bones turn to jelly for no reason."

He frowned. "Do you worry about these things, Bob?"

"All the time," I said. "But you don't, right? And you don't feel any pain. And you're as strong as an elephant. So it must be fun, eh?"

He smoothed down the duct tape over his wrist.

"I don't know that much about fun," he said.

"That Dr. Bernstein you were talking to on the phone just now—he's like your foster dad, right? So he's no fun?"

"He's with the army. He's in charge of us—him and Dr. Miller. And he's not fun."

"Us?" I said.

"I mean the house."

Imre's eyes were pools of gloom. I remembered that he'd lost his whole family.

"Sorry," I said. "I'm an idiot."

I felt kind of—I don't know—but then Evil-O hurtled down the basement stairs and grabbed a controller.

"Come on, you guys, I want to kill somebody!" she shouted. Death Squads is her favourite game. She managed to get us both before dinner.

Mom served us in the dining room with a tablecloth and candles, like it was Thanksgiving. She put Imre beside her and kept asking if there was anything she could do for him. Dad told her to leave the boy alone, and she said that it wasn't every day that her son brought home a friend like Imre.

"You mean a zombie, Mrs. Fuller," Imre said.

Mom gasped, and then caught herself.

"I'm sorry. It's shocking for me to hear such a demeaning word. But not when you use it. I guess that's your point, isn't it? It's *ironic*."

Imre was stabbing at the chicken with his fork.

"I've been reading all about you, to educate myself. *Pedes mortuus* is Latin and it means 'walking dead.' I want you to know that my friends and I are one hundred percent behind you in your struggle. You have every . . . every . . ."

Her voice trailed away as he began to chew, dribbling bits of food and sauce out of his mouth. Mom wiped her own mouth, which didn't need it, and looked away.

After dinner we went outside. Still some light in the sky, wet smells. The Foubert kids were playing kick the can. Samantha came over and stared at Imre.

"You hit Razor," she said. She pronounced it *Wayzah*.

He nodded.

"I hate Razor," she said.

She giggled and ran back to her family.

A green Jeep with tinted windows pulled up to us a few minutes later. Imre's ride. Two seconds after the door closed behind him something inside crashed against the window hard enough to crack the glass. I jumped back. There were growls and groans, and someone said, "No!" in a loud voice. The vehicle took off with a squeal and the smell of burnt rubber.

Evil-O and I stared at each other.

"Did you *hear* that?" I said. "That wasn't Imre. Aren't you scared? I'm trembling. Feel my pulse. Go on, feel."

The Jeep was at the end of the block. A window rolled down and a duct-taped hand came out and flapped a good-bye.

We waved back, a bit hesitantly.

CHAPTER 22

Next morning was a wet one. Grey clouds hanging low, heavy mist that was almost rain. Trees dripping. Evil-O's skateboard left a wake behind it when she rolled through the puddles. She told me about a dream she'd had where Imre was pointing at things with a stick and Susan Berdit was running around doing what he told her.

"What do you think, Bob?"

I thought, why was she dreaming about Imre? But that's not what I said.

"Sounds like Imre was class president."

Evil-O staggered off her board and turned to stare at me, up to her ankles in water. I wore boots because of the puddles. I like to keep my feet dry.

"Bob! You are a genius."

"I am?"

We were at the corner of Ewing and Westwood. I could

see the protesters and TV cameras in front of the school. "You're right—Imre *should* be class president."

"I was talking about your dream. No one would vote for him."

"Yes, they will. They will. They will!"

And she was off, pumping and wheelie-ing all the way to the end of the block, ripples of green water fanning behind her.

She sounded so sure of herself that I almost believed her. Evil-O is good that way. Once in kindergarten she convinced me that I was invisible. "Bob, Bob, where did you go?" she asked, looking right through me. I climbed onto the teacher's desk to grab a handful of reward jelly beans. "You can't see me," I said, stuffing my mouth as Miss Honey called my name. Miss Honey could see me. And I had to spend recess in the time-out chair. Evil-O laughed about that for years.

Mrs. Stinson was throwing her hands in the air and yelling, "Injustice" and "Trust us" and "Even if you bust us" when I hurried past. Mom and her friends were nodding their whole bodies forward, calling out, "Yes!"

Their opponents, the anti-Imre protesters, shouted: "Zombie, no, zombie, no." Or maybe it was "No zombie, no zombie." A noise like thunder overhead. News helicopters hovering.

Evil-O dragged me over to Imre, who had just arrived. His bus was backing down the drive.

"Tell him, Bob."

"Tell him what?"

"That we want him to run for class president. He doesn't believe me. It was Bob's idea, you know," she said.

"You're making fun of me," he said. "Of course you are. Ha ha. Zombie for class president. Very amusing. I'll put it in my diary. 'Today, Evil-O and Bob asked me to be class president. I am starting to fit in at Westwood Elementary.'"

We were under the overhang at the front of the school. A photographer standing on the street yelled at us to smile.

"What about you, Evil-O?" said Imre. "I do not want to take away from your chance to be president."

"Presidents are symbols, Imre," said Evil-O. "You're a more important symbol than I am. I'm happy to vote for you instead of running. And if *you* get elected, it'll mean that *they* lose." She pointed at the protesters. "Do you want *them* to win, with their bigotry and prejudice? If you can become president, it means that there's a chance for all the kids like you."

"You mean all the zombies?" he said. "You think that's what this world needs? More zombie presidents?"

I laughed.

"Bob!"

"What? It's funny. Imre's a funny guy. In addition to being strong and dead."

But a president? I honestly didn't think so. I pictured a zombie in a suit, lurching down the street, fresh blood dripping from his open mouth. People would ask, *Who elected him?*

Car horns brought me back to the present. Imre's bus had stalled while it was backing out of the school. The front end of the bus was still in the school driveway and the back stuck all the way across Westwood Avenue, so traffic was blocked in both directions. That's why the horns. TV guys were filming. Anything to do with Imre was news.

Evil-O snapped her fingers. "Got an idea."

I recognized the flash in her eyes. "Like when we were playing with my castle set and you tried to fire the toy cannonballs from the toaster? That kind of idea?"

"Shut up, Bob. It's about what you said about Imre being strong as well as funny. Strong is cool, right?"

"I don't know," I said. "Calvin is strong but I wouldn't vote for him."

"If Imre is going to be elected we have to show everyone what he can do."

She grabbed his sleeve and led him away. I started to follow, but when we got close to the school fence, one of the news people said, "Hey, there's the mystery girlfriend!" Another one said, "Put your arm around Imre! And smile!"

I turned and walked off by myself. I admired Evil-O's ideas even when they didn't work (smoke poured out of the toaster and my mom called 911), but I didn't want to hear any more girlfriend talk.

The honking had stopped. People leaned out of car windows, snapping pictures of the lines of traffic and the TV crews and the protests for and against Imre. I was watching them rather than what was happening on the driveway, so I missed the actual *lift*. I've seen it since, of course, hundreds of times. I have a copy of the *Time* magazine cover framed on my wall. But I did not witness the moment when Imre picked up the bus. I was facing away. What I remember is everyone else's reaction. They saw Imre, and I saw them as they realized what he was doing. A hundred faces all turning together, a hundred mouths opening, a hundred eyes popping. Make that two hundred. Dozens of cameras and cell phones pointing, clicking. A CNN guy saying, "Holy —— ," and a really bad word into his microphone, then clapping his hand over his mouth as if he thought he could keep the word in.

When I turned, the oversized front bumper of the bus was already well off the ground, and the vehicle was rolling slowly forward.

Imre was upright but bent slightly, with the bumper and the front part of the frame on his back. He was walking slowly, pulling the bus off the road and up the driveway.

I stared the way you stare at something you totally don't expect and can't yet understand. A Martian. A magic trick. A full-sized statue of Elvis made out of macaroni. The way the first person to see a giraffe must have stared.

Holy —— is right.

Imre's bus driver wore an army uniform with three stripes on the sleeve. He was talking into a walkie-talkie when I got there.

"Subject has school bus on his shoulders and is walking. Repeat, on his shoulders. He says he is okay. Over."

Evil-O was right next to Imre, bent at the waist, encouraging him. She was not the only one. There was a growing group of kids clustered around him, shouting, "Go, go, go!" I heard a roar from overhead—the helicopter was hovering lower than usual.

Step by step by step, the bus moved steadily up the school driveway. I thought of those nature shows where an ant carries a gigantic leaf. When the back end was well clear of the road, Imre bent forward, letting the weight off his shoulders. The front of the bus dipped, and Imre crawled out from under it.

The crowd was silent for a moment and then started to applaud. It was a release of tension. We'd all been holding our breath and now we could let it out. Maybe some people were freaked out by the stunt—hey, I was freaked out myself—but that just made it more satisfying to let go now it was over. The clapping got louder, and turned into shouting and finger-whistling and honking that spread across the schoolyard and down the street, where it rose in the air like fireworks, drowning the sound of the bell.

In a small town, school days last forever. Your reputation sets like cement. Win a championship, pee your pants onstage, fall off the roof in front of everyone, and people will talk about it for years. Mrs. Dithyramb is a grandma now but she got her tongue stuck to the flagpole when she was in the second grade. I know the story—it's part of town legend. Now take that idea and multiply it a million times because it was totally weird and totally awesome and the international media was on hand, and you have Imre lifting the bus. No one who was there that day would *ever* forget it. We'd talk about it forever.

"Thanks, Doc. You news folks can use that in your stories. Tell the world. Dresden, Ontario, is a safe and friendly town. Now, who wants to get the ball rolling here? There's a microphone up at the front. Yes, sir, you can go first."

Was Z-1 Imre's official name? I wondered. If he got married, would the preacher say, *Do you, Z-1, take this woman…?* He sat with his head tilted to one side, listening politely. He was handling the whole thing really well.

The guy at the mic said he was from New York. He asked Imre about lifting the bus. How did it feel? Was it hard? Could he do it again?

He held out a tape recorder.

"Sure," said Imre.

The reporter asked if he had always been strong.

Imre shook his head. "Only since…"

He paused.

"Since you died?"

"Yeah. Since then."

The guy beside me sneezed loudly. I don't like tuna fish very much. I turned away and promised myself a rinse with disinfectant when I got home.

Susan's mom was next up. When she called Imre a zombie, the right side of the hall applauded. The left side didn't. My mom—you can always hear your mom in a crowd—shouted, "Shame!" The mayor got everyone to shush.

"Come on, Mary Lee, this is a public forum and there are children here," the mayor said. "And we've just heard how young Imre is not dangerous. Can you put it a different way?"

Mrs. Berdit waved her hand. "Fine," she said. "How about

The Dresden town hall was packed the way I pack my suitcase. Mom tells me I don't need all that hand sanitizer and so many extra clothes on a weekend trip, but I say, "What if it rains? And what about restaurant bathrooms, have you *seen* them?" And she sighs and sits beside me on my bulging case so I can zip it up. *Full* is what I mean—the hall was full of people. I knew most of the faces from school or the mall or Main Street, but there were cameras and stage lights and lots of strangers. Mom and Dad walked down the centre aisle arguing about when we should have left and whose fault it was and I ducked away, ending up at the back between an old lady in a wheelchair and a guy who smelled like tuna salad.

The mayor was onstage fiddling with the microphone. She's a fat lady with a laugh, been mayor forever. Grey hair in braids down her back and a shirt with snaps for buttons.

"Okay folks, let's get started," she said, her words bouncing off the panelled walls and high ceiling. Behind her sat Buz and the superintendent, and a stranger fidgeting with his phone. All I could see was his glasses—big ones with thick black rims. Beside him was an empty chair.

The mayor thanked everyone for coming out. She was sure we'd rather be at home with a beer and a ball game but this was an important issue and the school board wanted to clear the air and she, the mayor, was happy to help.

She put her hands on her hips and paused.

"Heckuva thing, hey?" she said, and got a laugh. "Here's this kid, this Imre, and he's got the town in an uproar. Protests and such. Bad words, ruffled feathers, circus acts! Dresden is news. Folks from all over the world want to know about us. My gal Felicia back at the office spends so much time with the phones and email that she can't go out for doughnuts. And that, my friends, is serious."

Another laugh. The mayor joined in, her gold tooth catching the light.

"So let's get to it. I'm going to introduce the folks onstage, and then you can ask them questions. We'll see if a little straight talk can help. We want to hear your concerns. We want you to tell us your feelings. The more we know, the better."

There was some murmuring, mostly from the right-hand side of the crowd. Susan's mom was sitting down at the front on that side. I'd seen her when we came in.

The mayor introduced Buz first, "even though most every-one in the room here knows him." She called Superintendent Nelson "a wonderful hard-working gal," which made the superintendent frown mightily.

The other guy onstage was sitting up straight. Und the goggly glasses he had a tight little mouth like a butto His face was red. I'd seen him before. When the mayor sai his name he nodded quickly, like he was agreeing. *Yep, I'1 Dr. Bernstein.*

The mayor looked around. "Darned if we're not missing our star," she said. "I saw him a moment ago. Doc, do you hap pen to know where ... Ah, there he is. Welcome, young fella."

Imre trotted onstage from the side, wiping his hands on his pants.

"Sorry," he called. "Even zombies have to pee."

The mayor began by asking Dr. Bernstein about this *pedes mortuus* syndrome. What was the deal with that? She understood that some folks were so afraid of it they were keeping their kids home from school.

"Tell us straight, Doc," she said. "How dangerous is Imre?" She smiled.

Dr. Bernstein didn't smile back. He didn't look like he could.

"The army has been monitoring subject Z-1 for over a year," he said. "He is not infectious. He has exhibited no anti-social behaviours. He is classified as a zero risk."

The doc had a hissy, crackling kind of voice. Like a snake, maybe, or bacon frying. I love bacon.

"So you're saying we're all safe," said the mayor.

"Yes."

"We can keep our kids in school. They can play with Imre. Living and undead together, like the banner says."

She pointed. The cameras followed her finger.

"Yes."

I call him a zomboy? That's what the news calls him. That's what he is on the Internet. Hundreds of thousands of people call him zomboy. Will that do?"

She was talking about the YouTube video *Zomboy Lifts Bus*. By the time I saw it there were already two hundred and something thousand hits.

More murmuring around the gym. Mrs. Berdit talked over it.

"Whatever he is, he's not human. He does not belong in the same school as my Susan! And do you know what he is doing? He is running for class president! Can you imagine? My little girl has such a big heart, and this zomboy is running against her and he has no heart at all!" She was practically spitting into the mic.

A lot happened here. There were boos and shouts. The mayor told everyone to hold their horses. Evil-O jumped onto her chair and pointed dramatically at Mrs. Berdit. (Don't think I hadn't noticed Evil-O before. Of course I had. She was down on the left-hand side. White hair band, button-down shirt, clenched fists.)

"*You're* heartless!" she yelled. "And Susan's going to lose the election!"

Her mom sat next to her with an *oh no!* look on her face. She tugged at Evil-O's pant leg, trying to get her to sit back down, and—well, that's pretty much all I remember of the town hall meeting.

||||

I woke up in the emergency ward with a doctor leaning over me. He had a pimple on his forehead. For a minute it was exciting and scary. I thought I was turning into a zombie. I'd be dead and super-strong and Evil-O would feel sorry for me. But it didn't last. Dr. Pimple took my temperature and said I might be getting a cold.

"Oh," I said.

"Do you remember what happened?" he asked.

"No," I said—a total lie. Jumping away from another tuna-fish-flavoured sneeze, I'd tripped and slammed my head against the floor, or maybe the wheelchair on the far side of me. An easy ten out of ten for embarrassment except that I was unconscious.

"Should I stay home from school tomorrow?" I asked.

"Because of your cold?" said the doctor. "Nah, you're fine. Your dad can take you home now." He took off his gloves and left my cubicle.

Dad was in a chair reading a magazine. He'd been there all along.

"Weren't you worried about me?" I asked him in the car. "I might have caught *pedes* what's-it-called syndrome."

He laughed.

"If you had that walking-dead syndrome I'd be worried about *me*," he said.

Thanks, Dad.

CHAPTER 24

The next day, crowds were lined up on both sides of Westwood. A few protest signs (SHOW US THE HEART! was a new one), but way more cameras. When the bus pulled into the schoolyard, the air was full of flashes. Imre stepped down into a ragged chorus of some boos but mostly cheers. A guy from across the street kept yelling, "Lift the bus!" The crowd laughed.

Mrs. Berdit was waving her sign in front of a cameraman from CITY TV.

"Excuse me, lady," he was saying. "I want to get a shot of the zomboy."

"He has no heart!" she cried.

"Sounds like my ex," said the CITY TV guy. "But heart or no heart he can lift a bus. Would you mind moving out of the way?"

Two million views. That was why there were more cheers than boos today. Lifting a bus isn't as important as curing cancer, but it films better. You don't see crowds outside a research lab shouting, *Cure cancer! Cure cancer!*

Imre's face almost lit up when he saw Evil-O, which made me feel grumpy. He was glad to see me too. He came over and told me what a nice time he had had at my house. "Please thank your mother for me," he said.

When he turned away, Calvin tapped me on the shoulder.

"I'm watching you, Fuller," he whispered. "I am never going to forget that you hit me with that sign."

"Not ever—not even when you're old and grey?"

"Shut up! You got your pet zomboy with you now, but someday you won't."

"And then?"

"And then *pow!*"

It was Mary Martin's birthday, and the joke of the day was, How many Zen masters does it take to change a light bulb? After the announcements, the two presidential candidates stood in front of our class. Susan was wearing a skirt, a sweater, and a snooty expression. Imre had that old-timey look about him—soot and ashes and poverty. Think Tiny Tim only without the crutch.

Sunshine poured into the room, making squares and diamond patterns on the walls and floor. Ms. Eiger erased the 4 on the board, and wrote a 3. Three school days until the election. She smiled at Susan, and frowned at Imre.

"It's . . . time to get to know our . . . candidates," she said. "I want . . . you to make an informed choice so . . . here is your chance, boys . . . and girls, we'll start . . . with Susan."

And Ms. Eiger settled slowly back into her chair.

Susan had a stack of notes in her hand. She stepped forward with a crisp nod.

"Good morning, everyone. My name is Susan, and I think I should be your class president because I know you, because I am intelligent, and because I am a leader. I know each and every one of you because I've been your classmate for years. I know that Debbie's favourite band is Forget You're Falling. I know that Andrew got 97 percent in math last year. And that Evil-O's mom works in a shoe store. Imre doesn't know any of these things. He doesn't even know your names. Imre, who's that?"

She pointed at Roy, the kid sitting behind Debbie. Roy's the kind of super-shy kid who never says anything. He got really sick a couple of years back, was gone for two weeks, and no one noticed. No one. He blushed like a tomato now, and slouched so low he practically disappeared inside his desk. Imre didn't say anything.

"That's not fair," said Evil-O. "Ms. Eiger, that's not fair. Imre just came here."

"Exactly my point." Susan's smile was as warm as Spam. "How can Imre speak for you when he doesn't even know who you are?"

She turned to the next page of her notes.

"Now, intelligence. My average last year was over 90 percent. I represented our school in the province-wide spelling bee two years ago. I don't want to make fun of Imre, but does anyone here think he is especially intelligent?"

Dakota laughed meanly. There were other smiles too. I remembered the *i* before *e* lesson.

"He knows things that you don't know," called Evil-O.

"Like about being *dead*? Yes. But how does that make him a good leader? I know we're not supposed to use"—she made air quotes—"the *Z* word, and I am not blaming Imre for being what he is. But he is not like us. A class is a team, and the class president is the team leader. How can he lead a team he does not belong to?"

A late-summer hornet flew in through the open window and began circling the front of the class. Susan batted it away with her speech notes.

"A president is the head and heart of the class," she said. "A president needs life, needs humanity. I have these things. Does he?"

She pointed. A dollop of drool had just slopped out of Imre's mouth, and he was wiping it on the shoulder of his shirt.

"Is *that* a class leader? Would you follow him? Does he even *look* like a leader?"

She had taken a lot of the punch out of Imre's fame. She should have stopped talking now. But she didn't. She tried to make one more point.

"Maybe I can't lift a bus," she said. "But I have a heart. I won't back down."

At just that moment the hornet flew at her. She let out a startled *yip* and took a step back. The hornet followed her.

She flailed with her notes and ran for the door. Instead of clapping, everyone laughed.

"How amusing," said Imre. "You said you would not back down, and then you did back down, after all."

I sympathized with Susan. The hornet was angry and determined and as long as my thumb. We were all on our feet by this time. Ms. Eiger was climbing slowly out of her chair.

"Calm . . . down, everyone. I . . . must ask you to control your . . . selves."

The hornet started swooping around her. She couldn't outrun it, like Susan. Ms. Eiger couldn't outrun an hour hand. We watched, horrified, as the insect landed on her outstretched arm, lifted its giant abdomen, and plunged in its stinger, like a needle at the doctor's office.

"Oh . . . help, oh . . . help!" Ms. Eiger collapsed slowly backwards. The kids in the front rows screamed and scrambled out of the way.

The hornet found Imre next. He hadn't moved, hadn't even altered his expression. The insect circled his head a couple of times before landing on his cheek and crawling towards his upper lip. Imre's smile broadened slightly. The hornet disappeared.

Everyone froze.

What had just happened? Where was the hornet? Imre's mouth moved like he was sucking on a peppermint. I could hear a faint buzzing and then I couldn't. Imre swallowed. There was a collective gasp. Someone said, "Awesome." I agreed. In a way, it was more awesome than lifting the bus because it was more possible. I could no more lift a bus than fly, but I *could* swallow a hornet—and just the idea made me squirm. Imre had actually *done* it.

Susan stood in the doorway, puffing like an old steam engine. Her hair was a mess, her face was sweaty, and her shirt had come untucked from her skirt. Imre had his hands clasped in front of him, and a polite half-smile on his face.

The bell rang for a fire drill.

CHAPTER 25

When we got back to class, Swarty loaned Imre her laptop, and he played the *Zomboy Lifts Bus* video for his election speech. Ms. Eiger went to the office because she wasn't feeling well and Swarty gave us silent reading until lunchtime.

I ended up being swept along to the cafeteria as part of a large group from our class. Evil-O was there too, so I was eating lunch with her for the first time in a long time. She nodded down the table at me.

Kids kept coming up to Imre to say they had seen him on TV or the Internet. No one used the *Z* word. One little guy actually said that he wished he could be like Imre, which was interesting since at that moment Imre was eating some chocolate pudding and getting it everywhere. Honestly, he looked like he had just been licking out an oil barrel.

||||

After lunch Gezink and I went to the far side of the playground to kick things through the fence. He'd hurt his toe and was hopping up and down with his hair flapping all over his face when Evil-O came over with a juice box and offered him some.

"This is great," Gezink said, after a long swig. "The three of us together. We're, like, best friends, eh? I mean I know you guys are best-best friends, but I am too, kind of. It's good to have best friends."

He pushed his glasses up. Evil-O and I carefully did not look at each other. We had never thought that much about Gezink. You know the guy you play with because you're kind of sorry for him or until someone better comes along? Gezink was that guy.

"What about Imre? He's pretty cool, eh?" said Evil-O.

"Sure, he is. Sure." Gezink nodded approvingly. "Not everyone likes him, but we do. Right?"

I kicked a stone through the fence.

"I don't know about *cool*," I said.

"Well, maybe not *cool* cool," said Gezink. "But kind of."

"Yeah, kind of."

Evil-O frowned at me.

"No, he's okay," I said. "I like Imre. I do. It's just ... well, he takes some getting used to. He's ... I don't know."

"Yeah," said Gezink.

"Well, I really like him," said Evil-O.

"Me too," said Gezink.

||||

Three kids from Swarty's grade six class ran around the playground, dragging Imre along and laughing like anything. They came over and collapsed on the ground giggling. Shannon and Katie and a guy I didn't know.

"Imre's funny," said Shannon. "He was carrying us all at once."

"I am a riot," he said. Totally deadpan.

We were headed back towards the school when a shout from behind made us turn.

"Hey! It *is* him!"

There's a municipal football field on the other side of the fence. A dozen guys had been running up and down all lunch hour. Now half of them were jogging towards us, taking a moment in the middle of their workout.

"I thought so. It's the zomboy!"

"Hi there, zomboy!"

Imre waved and smiled, and the players jogged back to the track. They wore white long-sleeved shirts with BUZZARDS on the back.

"Hey, hey," said Evil-O, punching Imre in the shoulder. "Look at you! That's our town football team. They're, like, celebrities. And they know you."

"Go Buzzards!" yelled Gezink. He ran up to put his arm around Imre. "I always said you were cool."

Evil-O shot me a *ha ha ha* look. I shrugged. I was concentrating on a little tickle I had just noticed in the back of my throat.

|||

I spent afternoon recess making campaign posters. Not that I was on Imre's team or anything, but he asked me specially and Evil-O was right there and I didn't know how to say no. Also, I did not want to run into Calvin in a *pow* mood, all by myself on the playground.

I started to draw a picture of a kid carrying a school bus but I had to change my plan. I am not a great artist. (One summer we took art classes at the library. When I drew a rocking chair the instructor thought it was a cat. "What's your cat's name?" she asked. I didn't have a cat but Evil-O jumped in before I could explain. "Cody," she said with a sad smile. "Bob had a cat named Cody who ran away and Bob's still real sad about it. Aw, that picture looks just like Cody, Bob!" I laughed so hard the instructor thought I was crying. She gave me a Tootsie Pop, which Evil-O and I shared on the way home.) My school bus did not look like anything except a hippo, maybe. I coloured over it and wrote ZOMBOY RULES! The letters were off-centre and spaced wrong. I may be the worst artist in the world.

We were making the posters in Swarty's classroom because Ms. Eiger was still feeling bad and hadn't come back. The room looks out on Westwood Avenue. I saw Imre's bus arrive early. Imre frowned at it. Eyebrows down, lips tight.

"Anything wrong?" I asked.

He shrugged. "Some things are not going well at home. You know."

"Everyone has weird stuff at home," said Evil-O. "Bob's parents fight all the time. My mom won't even call me by my right name."

"I do not have parents. But there is disagreement."

"What about?"

He did not answer.

Evil-O finished her poster. She'd drawn a ballot with an X next to Susan's name. Underneath was the slogan DON'T DO THIS!

Evil-O was a good hater.

We went to the hall for a drink of water. "I didn't understand the joke from this morning," said Imre. "Why *does* it take one Zen master to change the light bulb, and one more to not change it?"

"It's sort of deep," I said.

"Sort of stupid," said Evil-O.

The announcement came right after the recess bell: "Evil-O Forester, Bob Fuller, and Imre Lazar to the principal's office immediately."

CHAPTER 26

Have you ever gone for a walk without thinking where you're going, letting one turn lead to another and another, and before you know it you find yourself in a place you never expected to be? It's like there is a force out there in the universe directing you.

I didn't want to be friends with Imre, but I'd been getting closer and closer for days now. He was best friends with my best friend, he had saved me from Calvin and Razor, he had eaten at my house. My mom carried a sign with his name on it. I was on a viral video standing next to him with a school bus on his shoulders. One blind turn after another, linking our names. Now that Imre was so famous, TV networks like the CBC wanted to do shows about him at his new school. When the school board said okay, the CBC asked Buz about Imre's friends. And the two names he came up with were Evil-O's and mine.

The head of CBC program development was in Buz's office when we got there. He jumped up from his chair when he saw us.

"Here they are!" he said. "The best friends! Great great great!" He came over, smiling like a chandelier. He shook Imre's hand first, then Evil-O's, then mine. He said *great great great* each time. My hand disappeared inside his. It was like shaking a pillow. He was a round ball of a guy with a buttoned sweater that barely met across his middle. Buz introduced us but I didn't hear his name. His voice was round, like him.

"What is going on in this school resonates through the world," he said. "You, Imre, are an explorer. You are Columbus, landing on an unknown shore, breaking new ground, forging new friendships. There's hardship. Prejudice. And Evil-O and Bob are reaching out, helping you. Especially you, Evil-O. I've seen you at his side. You're his champion! Maybe more, hey? A hint of romance? This story needs to be told. The country must know—hang on!"

Something was ringing from under his sweater. He pulled out a cell phone. "Not now," he said into it. "I'm with someone more important than you."

The plan was to follow us around for a couple of days, film-ing us as we hung out together at school and (I gulped—I couldn't help it) at Imre's place. Because we were all minors the CBC needed parental consent, which was why my mom and Mrs. Forester were there. Imre was a ward of the nation, and the CBC had a consent form signed in Ottawa for him. Filming would start next week.

The fat man wanted us to know that it was our show. "If there's anything you kids are worried about, say so!" he said.

I was worried, all right. I had worry like poison ivy, which I caught a couple of summers ago playing in the forest near Grandma's. (One of the worst cases Dr. Sophie had seen in fifteen years of doctoring, she said, with my legs and arms covered with golf-ball-sized blisters of pure golden poison.) I did *not* want to hang around while the CBC filmed Imre and Evil-O being friendly. Hint of romance, *yeesh*! I could imagine the movie director getting them to hold hands or something. I didn't want to pretend to be having fun while that was going on.

All this time, my mom was standing with her hands clasped and her lips parted like she was watching a miracle. Her son wasn't a bigot anymore. I had crossed over. I was changed, different, washed clean.

I wanted to shake her.

Funny, considering how happy my mom was about me, that Evil-O's mom was frowning as if her worst fears about her daughter were being confirmed. "Who is going to watch this show?" she whispered to my mom.

I couldn't tell how Imre felt. He looked pretty much like he always did.

"This documentary could help with your election," Evil-O told him. "Susan isn't going to—"

"*Stop!*"

The fat man threw his hands in the air.

"*What* election?" he asked.

Evil-O told him. As she talked, the fat man's eyes grew wider and wider and his mouth worked itself into different shapes. He was having a fit.

"An election!" he shouted. "The symbol of freedom and democracy. I was wondering how to shape the story, and this is the way. An election! Oh, it's great great great! It's perfect! I have to tell my people right away!"

He pulled out his cell phone as the last bell rang.

We drove Evil-O's mom back to work, with me and Evil-O in the back seat. There was a parking spot on King Street right in front of the Happy Feet store and Mom pulled in. Before getting out of the car, Mrs. Forester leaned over the seat to talk to her daughter.

"So you want to be on TV with your freak friend?"

"Mom, he's—"

"I'm not happy, Olive. You know I'm not."

Evil-O didn't say anything.

"I'm sure there isn't anything to worry about, Beth," said my mom. "This is the CBC, after all. Our national network. And Evil-O is a wonderful girl."

"Don't you think I know that? I know that. I know you're a wonderful girl, Olive. But people talk. Mr. Terwilliger called me into his office today to show me a picture of you and the—you and Imre in the *Dresden Evening Guide*. Everyone in town gets that paper, Olive. All our customers."

More than two million people had seen Evil-O with her arm around Imre. Dozens, maybe hundreds, were watching her at this very moment. Did Mrs. Forester know that? Old people are funny.

Then she said something even funnier.

"At least you aren't alone. Bob is friends with the freak too."

"I know. Isn't it wonderful?" said Mom.

Evil-O dug her nails into my arm. It was all I could do not to scream.

"The Fullers have lived in this town a long time," said Mrs. Forester, "and Bob has a good head on his shoulders. He's the only reason I'm letting you participate."

She slammed the car door and walked heavily across the sidewalk.

"Oh dear," said Mom.

She pulled out into traffic. Evil-O was twisting the consent form in her hands, wringing it out like it was a washcloth.

"If you say something nice to me, Bob, I'll punch you," she said.

I was thinking about how nobody really knows what anyone else is thinking.

CHAPTER 27

For me, the best part of the weekend is what it isn't: school. No bells, no gym class, no pioneers. (Hate those guys. We have them every year like head-lice inspection. Log cabins, homemade clothes, and candles and soap and fun. Olympically boring. *Pay attention, Bob!* Swarty used to say, and I would regretfully return from a fantasy where cool pioneers were knitting rocket ships to invade Mars.)

Evil-O and I played Death Squads and ate sandwiches on paper plates. Gezink came over and we tied a skipping rope to my bike and pulled each other on Evil-O's skateboard, which was fun until Gezink fell off and hurt his wrist.

By the end of the weekend Imre's YouTube video had six million hits on fourteen different postings. We watched it three or four times. I wanted to ask Evil-O how come she liked Imre so much. What did he have that I didn't have? *I've got a pulse,* I wanted to say. *And if you hold my hand it'll stay on.* But I kept this to myself. Scared, I guess. I was happy that we were friends again and I didn't want to wreck it. I did notice that she had soft brown hairs on her forearms, darker than the hair on her head.

Saturday night we rode our bikes to the mall and ran into Mrs. Good tying Razor up. The dog lunged at me. I jumped back and dropped my ice cream sandwich. Mrs. Good walked into the mall, laughing. The dog strained against his leash. Could he get free? The knot did not look very tight. Evil-O gave me half her ice cream but it's never the same, sharing. You want your own.

Sunday morning wasn't as good as Saturday morning. And by Sunday afternoon I was doing homework. Sunday at three thirty is the saddest time of the week. Worse than Monday. Really, the school week has started, only you don't know it yet.

Mom came back from a walk that evening with news from the Furillos. Something had broken into the chicken coop behind their market up on Highway 2 and killed all their birds. Feathers and blood everywhere, and the bodies had been torn to pieces. Mrs. Furillo said it must have been a whole pack of coyotes.

CHAPTER 28

It's hard to walk down the street with a video camera inches from your right cheek. I kept turning to look at it, and Melvin kept telling me not to. We were walking down the sidewalk in a clump, me and Evil-O, Melvin and the soundwoman and the cameraman.

Melvin was the director. He was long and skinny and talked like a computer. "Hello, Bob. Hello, Evil-O. Let us begin now. Do not look at the camera."

Our walk to school was a fake. We were pretending to walk at normal speed but it was taking us forever. After a half hour we were just turning onto Westwood. Good thing we started early.

"Hey, look at the people!"

Evil-O pushed forward on her skateboard, keeping a slow steady speed so that the camera could follow us easily. She was good at this filming stuff.

"They're carrying signs!" she said.

"Yeah! Signs," I said. I realized how dumb this sounded. I tried to think of something to add. "They sure are . . . *there*."

I could hear a very quiet chuckle near my right ear. The cameraman. Not the first time he'd laughed at me. His name was Johnny. He was okay.

"Sorry," I said.

"Do not look at the camera," said Melvin.

"Poor Imre," said Evil-O. "Imagine having to face angry people every time you go to school."

"Yeah," I said. "Imagine that."

"I'd hate it."

"Yeah," I said. Again.

Whatever I said sounded lame. I wished I had a script. Life would be easier with a script, don't you think? Improv is hard. No wonder movie stars always seem so cool. It isn't just the sunglasses. It's the scripts.

"What?" I said to Evil-O.

"I asked you about the class election, you idiot."

"Hey, is she allowed to call me an idiot?"

"Do not look at the camera, Bob," said Melvin. "How often must I tell you?"

Johnny filmed the protesters, for and against. Susan's mom was screaming. My mom and Mr. Jin were swaying earnestly. Mrs. Stinson was in the middle of a new rap.

Zomboy not a tomboy, he's a bomb
Does the work

Clean and jerk, with a bus
No muss or fuss,
No need for a truss—

I heard Melvin ask Johnny if he was getting this and Johnny said, "Oh yeah." The soundwoman was off to one side, pointing her boom microphone.

When Imre got off the bus, someone in the crowd shouted for him to lift it. I wondered how long it would take for people to get sick of that. The film crew followed him as he walked towards me and Evil-O.

"Act natural," she muttered.

Imre looked even gloomier than normal. Evil-O went up and punched him on the arm.

"Hey! How's the future class president?"

She was good—you couldn't miss how much she liked him. She gave me a *come on* gesture. Like, *say something!* The camera was a lizard's eye. I gazed into it, hypnotized. *Act natural*—but I didn't know what that meant. Could I ask Imre what was wrong? Was that a natural thing to ask?

A script, I thought. My kingdom for a script.

"Lift the bus!" someone shouted.

Evil-O was looking past my shoulder. Two guys and a girl stopped in front of us. One of the guys lived over on Beattie Crescent, behind my place. The other was Andrew's little brother, Leo, who winked at me. Didn't he know I was mad at him?

"What do you think of our outfits?" he asked.

Black, baggy clothes. Belts that hung down. Dark circles under their eyes.

Evil-O got it first. She snapped her fingers.

"You're dressed like Imre!" she said.

"Yup. We're zomboys," said Leo.

They marched off, swinging their arms. Johnny filmed the whole thing.

When the bell rang, we moved across the playground together. Evil-O walked with her shoulders back and her head up. The sun made her hair gleam. Her eyes were shadowed, dark and deep-set. Her mouth was wide, her chin long and strong. I found myself holding my breath, my heart beating too fast for me to count.

CHAPTER 29

We had a substitute teacher that day. Her name was Miss Howe. She blinked a lot. Dry eyes, probably. I knew all about that. Buz must have told her about the filming, because she didn't seem surprised to see the CBC people. When the announcements were over (choir practice; lost jacket; Ann Arthur's birthday; What do Winnie-the-Pooh and Alexander the Great have in common?), she took attendance. Johnny filmed that.

She knew about the election too. She had changed the number in front of the DAYS LEFT sign to 2.

Susan welcomed Miss Howe to the school, "on behalf of the rest of the class," and said her dress looked very stylish. That was Susan's word—*stylish*. She asked if she could hand out some treats, and before Miss Howe could say yes or no, she and Debbie and Dakota were running around the class with cookies.

Not a bad way to start the week, you know—cookies. They were oatmeal with sprinkles in the middle that spelled out SUSAN.

"Hey!" said Evil-O. "You're bribing the class to vote for you. That's not fair!"

"Bribing?" Susan smiled. "No, Evil-O. I'm campaigning. A good president takes care of her class. Would anyone like another cookie?"

"What are you doing, Bob?" yelled Evil-O.

"What?" I had my hand up. "These are good."

The CBC guys had finished packing up their stuff. Before following Melvin out the door, Johnny leaned close to me. "You're hilarious, kid," he said.

Evil-O asked to have the window open.

"I'd like to let in some fresh air," she said. "I'm feeling warm."

"I wonder if anyone else is feeling warm?" asked Miss Howe.

"No!" said Susan. "No, no! Keep the window closed!"

Of course she was thinking about the hornet. The class laughed.

Dakota turned sideways in her chair. "What're you doing, Evil-O?" she demanded.

"Campaigning," said Evil-O.

For geography class, Miss Howe had us make up a phrase to remember the names of the continents. You know, like *Never Eat Shredded Wheat* for north, east, south, and west. I finished mine and then it was recess.

I went over to Imre and asked him what was wrong.

"You look awful." I almost added *even for you* but caught myself. "Is it the TV thing?"

He nodded.

"They will be filming at our house today and Dr. Bernstein is very upset. He thinks that you and Evil-O and the TV cameras will disturb the experiment."

I couldn't help gulping again—an inside gulp—at the idea of going to Imre's place. But he looked so unhappy I wanted him to know I was on his side. Also, I didn't understand.

"Aren't *you* the experiment?" I asked. "You're the one going to school, getting back to being a regular guy after—everything. What's wrong with having visitors?"

Imre didn't say anything.

"Dr. Bernstein didn't mind you coming to my house for dinner," I went on. "Why doesn't he want us going there?"

Overhead, the sun was playing leapfrog with a line of clouds. Around us, kids were screaming and throwing things. Leo and his friends, the pretend zomboys, walked arm in arm in arm across the playground like they owned it.

"Is this anything to do with what happened when you got picked up at my place?" I said. "There was something else in that green Jeep, wasn't there?"

"I can't say. I mean, I can't tell you. It's a secret."

I wanted to run over to Evil-O and say, *I told you so! I knew there was something weird going on! Maybe next time you'll believe me!* I didn't, though.

I patted Imre on the shoulder.

"Secrets suck," I said. He nodded.

Something caught in the weave of his shirt came out when I patted him. White and fluffy, it swirled in an air current before floating gently to the ground. A feather.

Aunt Agatha Ate Alligators, Some Alligators, Not All, Ew.

That was my memory sentence for the continents: Africa, Australia, Antarctica, Asia, South America, North America, Europe. Though I guess you could mix up the first ones: Australia and Africa, say. The substitute teacher didn't put my sentence on the board. She liked Susan's better.

Aliens And All Scary Awful Nightmares Are Actually Evil.

"Isn't a grammatical sentence more fun to read?" said Miss Howe.

"Oh yes," said Susan. "And it's instructive too. Aliens *are* evil."

She glared at Imre and sat down.

"Does anyone else have a sentence they would like to share with the class?" asked Miss Howe.

Evil-O stood up, and spoke carefully, with spaces between the words.

"Susan. And. Her. Friends. Are. Cows. And. Should. Keep. Their. Mouths. Shut."

Miss Howe frowned, chalk in hand. "But those aren't the right letters for the continents."

"No," said Evil-O. "No, they're not."

CHAPTER 30

School was done and the three of us stood beside the far fence, waiting for Imre's bus and watching the Dresden Buzzards run laps in full equipment. The zomboy dress-alikes were tossing a Frisbee around on their way out of the playground. One of them threw wildly. The disc hit Imre flush in the face, bounced off, and rolled away.

"Wow!" yelled the girl. "I am *so* sorry."

"No, no. It was my fault. My forehead got in the way of your throw."

The Frisbee rolled through the gap in the fence and onto the track. Imre went after it without noticing that four or five guys in shoulder pads—a small flock of Buzzards—were heading straight for him. They must not have seen him because they ran into him without stopping. For a few seconds I lost sight of him under their arms and legs and jerseys and helmets. Next thing I knew, the players were lying on the ground and Imre was standing on the track with the Frisbee under his arm. We hustled over. The Buzzards were getting up slowly. The one with the beard limped to the grass and sat down. Imre was untouched, unruffled. He put up his hands in a *my bad* gesture.

"Sorry," he said. "Sorry, everyone."

Leo punched me on the arm. "Did you see that, Bob? Did you see that? Imre knocked those big Buzzards over. All of them."

The coach stood in the middle of the field. His whistle had fallen out of his mouth. He gave Imre a long look. You could see his mind working.

The bus driver was in the army—short hair, camouflage, boots.

"Bravo 5 to Bravo 1," he said into his headset as we started off. "I have Z-1 plus two more. Over."

He nodded to himself at whatever Bravo 1 was telling him, and said, "Roger. Over and out."

Army talk.

We sat in the middle of the bus. No one else was there that I could see. I checked. Evil-O sat next to Imre. I sprawled in the seat ahead, back to the window, feet up.

I just had to ask again: "Was there someone else with you on the first day of school, Imre? Or some*thing* else?"

"I told you, Bob, I can't say. It's a secret."

"Was it the same someone who was in the Jeep that came to pick you up from my place?"

I thought Evil-O might tell me to leave Imre alone but she didn't. She wanted to know too.

Imre looked worried and didn't answer.

The sun was in front of us and a bit to the left. This was the way to Hope Springs, where my grandma lived and I got poison ivy that time. We passed the Canadian Tire and the carpet place and a couple of cornfields. We came to Furillo Family Farms. The sign out front said GET YOUR FARM-FRESH EGGS HERE. I thought about the dead chickens and the feather on Imre's shirt. Coincidence? Part of the secret?

We turned down a lane I'd never noticed. Trees on one side, fields on the other, and three soldiers blocking our way. The nearest one spoke to our driver and then stood back to let the bus through. The lane ended in a big circle, where the bus turned and the doors opened. Two CBC vans were there already.

"Goodbye," I said to the driver. "I mean, roger, over and out."

He just looked at me. Army guys have no sense of humour.

The air smelled of animal poop and grass and pine needles. Mostly animal poop. My hands were damp and my breathing and pulse were spiking. And for good reason. I was walking up to an old farmhouse in the middle of nowhere with a zombie. I wiped my hands and tried to smile.

"Nice fence you have here, Imre," I said. "Very secure. Look at the size of that NO TRESPASSING sign. You are *not* messing around. You do not want any trespassers."

"Are you okay, Bob?" said Evil-O.

"Me? Fine. Sure. Totally."

How could she sound so calm?

I noticed a small hole in the fence, near the gate. Like a dog had dug under it.

There was a dead tree at the front corner of the house, with branches sticking out at odd angles. The house itself extended way back. There was a weather thing on one of the roof points—an arrow swinging in the wind. What are they called again? Anyway, one of them. A sudden gust of wind sent the pine trees flailing and the arrow thing spinning around. A crow flew by, black wings flapping against the sun, cawing hoarsely.

Spooky much?

The front door opened and a crowd of people poured onto the porch. Melvin and Johnny and the fat man and the soundwoman and some others. Johnny had the camera on his shoulder. The fat man called us the three musketeers and said it was great great great to see us. I followed Evil-O and Imre into the house, and met the army scientists who weren't his parents. Dr. Bernstein had the same big glasses and tight mouth I remembered from the meeting in the town hall. He was not happy to see us. Dr. Miller gave us a faint smile but she didn't mean it.

The place was bright and bare. Lots of extra lights on stands, with cords and cables trailing all over the floors. I made sure to stay with people. If there was a creepy secret in the house, I didn't want to find it. You know the girl in the horror movie who wanders upstairs alone to check out the funny noise? Not me. But I was hungry. I asked if there was anything for a snack.

"I don't usually eat snacks," said Imre.

I stared at him. "No?"

We went to the kitchen to check. The long table was old, the wood worn as smooth as glass by generations of elbows. There was a tired old quilt on the wall and a tired old high chair off in the corner. I could imagine the hungry family gathered around me, tucking into roast beef and apple pie. There'd be a baby in a bib and someone would have to help Grandma cut her meat. It was all so vivid. Man, I could practically smell the . . .

Wait, what did I smell?

"Do you have a dog?" I asked Imre. He and Evil-O were peering into the fridge.

"I can smell dog food," I said.

"There's dog food in here," she said. "An open can. Along with some cheese and a whole shelf of pills and a bag of—"

"Supplies that are none of your business," said Dr. Bernstein, reaching past her to close the fridge door.

I hadn't noticed him. He moved like mist.

"Do you want some dog food, little girl?"

"Uh, no thank you," said Evil-O.

"Are you sure?"

"Yes."

"Then why don't you go away."

He stared us out of the kitchen. Dark eyes behind those enormous glasses. A rounded flushed face, full of blood. I remembered that later.

CHAPTER 31

They filmed us talking about the election. First we were playing Twister, then we were sitting at the kitchen table. Evil-O was so enthusiastic with the spinner. "Left foot green!" she shouted. "Come on, you guys! Pretend you're stomping on Susan Berdit's head!" Which made me laugh out loud, and Imre looked surprised, and we had to try the scene again. There was one gross bit a few minutes later when I looked down and saw an ear sitting on a coloured green circle. Imre's, of course. The soundwoman gagged.

Melvin told us to take a break. The soundwoman left the room, and Dr. Miller stepped forward with some clear tape.

When we set up in the kitchen I thought I was finally going to get something to eat, but no. There were plates of cheese and crackers for us but Melvin told me not to put anything in my mouth.

"You are only pretending to eat, Bob."

"*What?*" I said.

Johnny smiled behind his camera.

"I want that cheese back when you are finished with it," said Dr. Bernstein, who had misted into the room along with us. He glared at us the whole time we were talking about votes. He'd glared at us through the Twister game too. When he wasn't glaring he was looking at his watch. Not a good host.

They set up the living room for interviews. Evil-O went first. Imre and I went upstairs to his room to wait our turn. I kept looking around for . . . I didn't know what. Something scary. If this was a horror movie, the music would be going *deedl deedl deedl*. If I was watching, I'd be sinking in my seat, getting ready to cover my face.

Imre had an iron bed and a cheap desk and chair. A bare bulb hung from the middle of the ceiling. No carpet, no pictures, no books, no games.

"Wow," I said. "Luxury city here."

He shrugged. "I don't need much."

"That's good."

I went over to the open window and leaned out. The twisted old tree at the front of the house had some branches that stretched back this way. There was one not far from the window. If Evil-O was here she would be trying to convince me to climb out the window and down the tree, and I would be saying, *I don't think so.*

The low afternoon sun made my eyes water. It glinted where it touched metal—the edge of the silo a few fields over, the top of the fence, the bars on the window next to Imre's window. I drew in my head.

His chair was one of those plastic ones on wheels. I sat down and pushed myself away from the desk. The wood floor was smooth and level, and I rolled almost to the far wall. Not bad, I thought. I chair-walked myself back and tried another push-off, getting all the way to the wall this time.

"You ever do this?" I said.

He shook his head. I rolled back to the bed and pushed off again, spinning myself around in the middle of the room. I counted five revolutions. The room was whirling when I tried to stand up.

"Wow! That was fun. You want to try?"

It was strange to see him thinking about it. I mean, it wasn't a big decision.

"Come on." I shoved the chair over to him. "It makes you dizzy," I said.

We traded places. His feet didn't touch the floor, so I pushed him over to the wall. It didn't take him long to get the hang of the spinning—a couple of tries and he had it. He was so strong that the chair spun like a top. I lost count of the revolutions. He was doing his odd, creaking laugh. When the chair slowed, his eyes were wide and round. He stood up and had to sit down again.

We tried a distance run, figuring the chair would go farther with both of us on it together. He sat on my lap since he was so much smaller. We faced away from the open door, all four of our feet on the opposite wall.

"Ready?" I said.

He nodded.

"Set?"

He smiled.

"Go!"

We pushed together, his little knees straightening inside mine. We rolled across the bedroom, out the door, and down the long upstairs hall. The floor was polished wood, and we coasted past bedrooms and bathrooms and I don't know what, spinning gently as we slowed, and finally coming to rest near the top of a second set of stairs.

Dr. Miller was coming up with an armful of laundry. "What are you two doing here?" she asked sharply.

Imre clambered off my lap. The laughter had gone out of him. Grown-ups will do that to you.

"We were just playing," I said.

"Stop it. Stop playing right now. They are looking for you downstairs. You have to go home," she said to me. "You and your friend."

The laundry moved.

I saw it, clear as paint. Dr. Miller was carrying what looked like bedsheets in her arms, and a large rounded bump appeared. I heard a faint growling sound.

The doctor shifted the load in her arms and bent towards it.

"No, Kato," she whispered firmly. "No!"

More growling. The doctor was wearing thick gloves. They went all the way up to her elbows. Without a word to us or a look back, she went down the hall and into the room next to Imre's, and shut the door firmly behind her.

CHAPTER 32

Johnny and Melvin and the rest of the crew were packing up one of the CBC vans. The fat man was on the phone, yelling at someone. Dr. Bernstein was watching from the porch with his hands on his hips. Imre and I went out onto the lawn. Still talking, the fat man got into the other van and took off. The sun was below the top of the treeline now, and the air was cooler. There were horses walking around in the field next door.

I thought about the growling bundle, and the broken window in the Jeep, and that weird pumpkin head in the bus window on the first day.

"Kato's a dog, right?" I said.

Imre didn't reply. He had a closed-in expression that was different from his usual gloom and nothing like the smile he'd had when we were playing on the chair. Home stuff was tricky, all right. And secrets were no fun.

"Is Kato dangerous? Is that why there are bars on the window?" I shuddered. I knew about dangerous dogs.

He swallowed without answering my question. "Please, Bob" was all he said.

For the first time ever, he actually looked upset. Kato was important to him. And that made me feel funny. I found myself caring about Imre. I didn't like dogs but he did, and there was something wrong with his dog and he felt bad.

"Okay," I said.

That was all. I stood there on the grass, smelling the horse poop, wondering how friendship worked. And realizing that it worked like this.

"No problem," I said.

"Thanks." His expression lightened. He punched me gently on the arm.

A moment later Evil-O came out, wiping her face. "I hate wearing makeup," she said. "Makes me feel like a clown."

She and I sat in the back seat of the CBC van on the way home. Evil-O said she thought it'd be a good idea if Imre handed out candy to the class.

"You hated Susan doing that," I said. "You said she was bribing people."

"Yeah, I know. But this is for our side. Do you have any candy?"

"No. And if I did, I wouldn't give it away."

"You're such a hog."

We passed the sign that said WELCOME TO DRESDEN,

POP. 17,500. (The sign on the other side of town said WELCOME TO DRESDEN, POP. 17,000. Go figure.)

"What did you and Imre do while I was on camera?" asked Evil-O.

"Huh? What? Nothing. Nothing at all," I said quickly. Too quickly? I took a breath, slowed down.

"I mean, uh, you know, the usual," I said.

"You're breathing funny."

"I am? Yeah, I am. I think my asthma is kicking in."

CHAPTER 33

L ift the bus!"

As usual, there was a huge crowd in front of the school the next morning. Down the block and up the hill. I had seen at least a dozen cars with strange licence plates on the way to school. People from Quebec and New York come to see Imre.

"Lift the bus!"

Johnny was filming from far enough away to get all of us in. Melvin stood beside him, telling him where to aim, pointing at the crowd, the bus, Mrs. Stinson—who was calling herself Rappin' ZED these days, and had started her own YouTube channel—Susan and her mom, and us.

"Lift the bus!" shouted somebody, even though it had already left.

Buz stopped us on our way to class. He was with the coach of the Dresden Buzzards—the guy who had watched his players run into Imre. At first I thought he was there to complain about Imre wrecking his practice, but that wasn't it at all. Turned out he wanted Imre to play for the Buzzards.

"Go Buzzards!" I just liked saying it. What a great name for a team.

"You are kidding, sir," said Imre. "I do not know anything about football."

"Knocked half my backfield down," said the coach. "Wade's still limping. Never seen anything like it."

"Try one game, Imre," said Buz. "See if you like it. Coach Awry and I have gone over the rules, and there's nothing that says you are too young to play. And football is a great game. I played for the Buzzards myself for a couple of years."

Imre looked at us. Evil-O nodded enthusiastically.

"Lazar the star!" she said in a loud voice.

Some kids heard this, and clustered over. When Evil-O told them what was going on, they cheered and ran off to tell their friends. I heard a couple of people yell, "Go Buzzards!"

"This is way better than candy or cookies," said Evil-O.

Susan carried her NO UNDEAD CLASS PRESIDENTS!! sign to class. Miss Howe, who was still filling in for Ms. Eiger, told her to put the sign away. "Inappropriate," she said. Susan flung it away and stomped to her desk. There was something a bit ragged about her today. A corner of the sign caught Gezink on the neck and he put his hand on the place.

"Darn it," he said.

Miss Howe changed the number on the blackboard from 2 to 1.

The daily joke at the end of the announcements was the same as yesterday's. Buz must read them off a list. Half the class yelled out the answer before he finished: "The same middle name."

Imre turned to me. "I understand that one," he said. "But I don't think it's funny. Maybe I only get part of it."

"Jokes are like soap bubbles," I said. "You don't get part of one."

Half an hour later, Miss Howe was onto her fourth number line, arrows pointing this way and that. She wanted to know what negative five plus four was. Andrew was waving his hand in the air and saying that he knew, he knew, he knew.

Imre broke his pencil again. He was always breaking his pencil, pressing too hard on the paper. He borrowed my sharpener.

One of his fingernails was covered in black gunk. Seriously creepy stuff. It couldn't be blood, could it? Dried blood? No, it was probably some kind of grease. I offered him my hand sanitizer, but he didn't know what to do with it.

"Here," I said, and held his hand while I squeezed. Then I used some myself.

"Thanks, Bob."

"Keep the bottle," I said.

"No, I—"

"Keep it."

He was the same strange-looking little guy he'd always been, and his hygiene was atrocious and Evil-O still thought he was the coolest. The difference now was, I kind of thought so too. I liked him. So he had mysterious stuff on his hands, so what? Grime and gloom and all, I liked him.

CHAPTER 34

The CBC crew had set up at my place. Our living room was hung with white sheets, lights on stands, and reflectors. I was sitting in a hard wooden chair. For this interview, Melvin would ask questions, and I would speak directly to the camera.

Ever since we'd started shooting the documentary, Mom had been all, *My son the movie star.* She watches *Inside the Actors Studio* on TV. "Are you being *in the moment?*" she kept asking me. Seems like actors always talk about being in the moment. I didn't know what she meant. What other moment could you be in?

When Johnny turned on the camera, I remembered Mom's acting advice and tried to be in the moment—that one right there. Except that as soon as I thought about one moment it was gone, and there was another moment to be in. And then that one was gone too. The camera's eye was dark, round, and deep, like a double-fudge brownie with hot chocolate sauce, candied nuts, and sprinkles—ohhhh, sprinkles, soft sweet flakes of heaven. You don't need them, but . . . wow.

"Is something the matter, Bob?"

"No no. No. This makeup feels funny, that's all."

(Yeah, I was wearing makeup. Go ahead, laugh. The woman who put it on told me I had really nice skin.)

"Please relax," said Melvin. "Tell me, who is your best friend?"

"Evil-O."

"Very well. Speak to the camera as if you are speaking to Evil-O. The camera is your friend, Bob. Are you ready? Then let us begin."

Melvin: How did you feel when you found out Imre was undead?

Me: I was grossed out. Kind of. I mean, it's creepy, right? And there aren't any other undead kids in my neighbourhood.

Melvin: So you were put off by Imre's differentness.

Me: Yeah, his differentness. You could say that.

Melvin: Now that you know Imre better, how do you feel about him?

Me: He's okay. We had fun playing at his place.

Melvin: He is running for class president and you are working on his campaign. Do you feel that he brings a message of hope?

Me: Hope for what?

Melvin: Under the skin, we are all the same. How do you get that message across to voters?

Me: It's not really true though, is it? Imre's got sludge in his veins and his hand is held on with tape.

Melvin: Stop.

He came out from behind the camera to explain what he wanted from me. The special was going to follow Imre on his quest for acceptance, he said, fighting prejudice in his run for class president.

"So you want me to talk about Imre being a regular kid? Just like me except that he can lift a bus, and bits and pieces of his body are held on with tape? Is that it?"

"Perhaps not about the tape," said Melvin. "But you can speak about the ways Imre is the same as you."

I said I'd try. Melvin checked with lights and sound and told Johnny to start rolling. The first question was about the campaign. And then I—well, I kind of blew it.

Melvin: So do you think there is something hidden about Imre? Or is he basically a boy like you?

Me: Hidden? Like a secret? What makes you say that? What kind of secret would Imre have?

Melvin: That is the point I wish to make. He is a boy like—

Me: Ha ha ha. Secret? Well, I guess we all have secrets, eh? I have this stash of candy in my closet that no one knows about except Evil-O—only now I guess everyone who's watching this knows too, eh? I'm going to have to move it. But I wouldn't know anything about Imre's secrets.

Melvin: Is something wrong, Bob?

Me: I mean, what secret would Imre have? His parents are dead. It's not like he has a mystery living with him. Hiding under a blanket or something. Now that would be a secret.

Melvin: What did you say?

Me: Nothing. I mean, I don't remember. I was just talking. Secrets? Mystery? Blanket? I don't remember what I said.

Melvin: Calm down, Bob. Act natural.

Me: Ha ha ha. Sure. Natural! Ha ha ha ha ha ha ha!

Melvin: Let's take a break now.

Evil-O called after dinner, wanting to know how the inter-view had gone. "Fine," I said. I didn't mention Johnny's tears of laughter. Or Melvin saying he never wanted to work with kids again.

CHAPTER 35

Dreams are funny things. They seem to make so much sense while you are in them, but when you wake up you think, what was *that* about?

I was standing in a castle dining hall, and there was all this amazing food—roast turkey stuffed with ice cream, spaghetti with caramel sauce, chocolate bars with Kentucky Fried Chicken inside, peanuts that exploded like gunpowder. Very cool. I had my dad's apron on, and Imre gave me a dish of dog food for Kato. I knew Kato was on my left but I couldn't turn my head that way. *Are you in the moment, Bob?* Imre asked. *What moment, Bob? Bob? Bob!*

Imre's mouth opened wider and I could see all his broken teeth. I was falling in. *Bob! Bob! Bob!*

I woke up. Evil-O stood at the foot of my bed dressed for school in a grey hoodie and jeans, her hair damp from washing.

"Bob! Get up!"

I took the corner of the pillow out of my mouth. Made a face.

"Another eating dream?" she said.

I sneezed. And sneezed. And sneezed again.

Buz had serious news for us that morning. Ms. Eiger was in the hospital in critical condition after developing a rare allergic reaction to the medicine they'd given her for the hornet sting. They didn't know if she was going to recover or not. "Our thoughts and prayers are with . . . her and her family," he said. The pause reminded me of the way Ms. Eiger used to talk. I don't know if he did it on purpose, or if it was just a coincidence. There was no daily joke.

I blew my nose for the thirty-ninth time that day. Oh, how I hate colds. Can't breathe, can't talk right. Can't taste—that's the worst.

Travis, the kid who sat in front of Calvin, was wiping his eyes. I wondered if Calvin had hurt him worse than usual, and then I remembered that Ms. Eiger was his aunt.

Imre spent the first period sighing. When he reached over to use my pencil sharpener, I asked if he was thinking about Ms. Eiger. With my stuffed nose it came out, *Thiggig*.

"Or the election?" I said.

He shook his head.

"Kato tried to get out again last night," he whispered. "I caught her just in time."

So Kato was a she, and she got out now and then. I remembered the dead chickens and the feather on Imre's shirt. Had Kato got out before?

"Well, that's good, isn't it? That you caught her?"

"I guess so."

"She's smaller than you, right? She might hurt herself." *She bight*, it sounded like. He didn't say anything.

Our usual lunch table was full—mostly kids from our class but some little kids as well. A lot of them were dressed like Imre, and they ate like him too—there were gobbets of food all over. Gezink was right beside Imre, his mouth sticky with banana, looking pleased as anything.

Evil-O came up behind me.

"I wonder how many people are watching Susan Berdit chew *her* cud?"

"Do I hear you calling Susan a cow?" I said.

"Moo."

We moved a couple of tables over. Travis plunked himself across from us and put his head in his arms. Evil-O looked at me like, *What do you say?*

"Sorry to hear about your aunt," I said.

I offered him a Kleenex, took a fresh one, and blew my nose. Tuna-fish sandwich for lunch and I wouldn't be able to taste it. Colds are hell.

"Aunt Ellie gives the best Christmas presents," said Travis. "Last year she got me a Medieval Action castle set, with a working trebuchet."

"I never knew her first name," I said. Ellie Eiger. It made her seem like a different person.

"And the presents are always neatly wrapped, with even edges and ribbons and such. And just now I was thinking, what if she dies? I'll never get presents wrapped that neat. Never again. That's what death means."

Travis gathered up his mostly uneaten lunch and wandered away. I dug into my tasteless sandwich. The noises of two hundred people eating lunch bounced around us like basketballs.

"Travis is lame," said Evil-O. "Medieval castle. Wrapping paper. Geez. Eiger was mean to Imre and I'm glad she's gone."

"Wow, that's cold."

She shrugged.

"One hornet sting," I said. "I guess we're all pretty close to death all the time, eh? Unless you're Imre. Then you're past worrying about it."

On instinct I checked my pulse—pretty good.

Travis and Imre were standing apart from the rest of the lunch table, talking seriously. Of course Imre would know about losing family. He put his hand on Travis's arm and nodded.

I thought about my grandma in Hope Springs. One birthday she gave me a human skeleton, three feet of grinning skull and jangly bones, the whole thing made out of hard white candy. It came with a stand, and I set it up on the kitchen counter and ate it bone by bone. Mom used to shudder but Dad would laugh every time I took off a piece of a rib or pelvis.

Never again, huh?

I blew my nose for the fifty-third time.

CHAPTER 36

Legion Field is on the east side of town by the water treatment plant. There's a parking lot and a booth that sells hot dogs and bags of chips and sweet fountain cola. The stands are on the parking-lot side of the field. From the top row you have a view of the long flat horizon of the lake, which is nice to look at when you have a hot dog in your hand and your team is doing badly, which the Buzzards often are. Last year they won one game and this year was supposed to be even worse (which was maybe why the coach was desperate enough to try Imre in the lineup). But so what? Your team is your team and Dresden loves the Buzzards.

By the time we arrived the parking lot was full, and we had to park down the block and walk back. Mom and Dad held hands. She was telling him he needed a haircut and he was saying *umph*. Evil-O and I ran ahead.

I took deep breaths. Was my cold worse? Did I feel the

same as I had at dinner? Or worse? I reached out and touched Evil-O's bare arm with my fingertips.

"What are you doing, Bob?"

"Checking my temperature." I grabbed her hand, put it on my forehead. "Feel."

She pulled away. "You are such a baby."

The home section of the stands was jammed with people I knew. There were lots of green shirts here—green was the Buzzards' colour. The far end of the stands was full of red Cougars shirts. The Cougars were from Hope Springs, up the highway from Dresden and a way better team—league champions for the past two years.

Johnny was filming the crowd. Melvin and the fat man were standing next to him. When he saw us, the fat man lit up like a flare.

"There you are!" he said. "Sit where Johnny can see you. Johnny, make sure you get these two cheering their friend. First Imre wins over the school and now he's playing for the town. Breaking the barrier, becoming a hero. And"—he lowered his voice—"we're the only ones here. We can sell the clips around the world if anything happens. 'Zomboy wins the game!' CNN or BBC or Indo-Asian News Service would kill for that." He chuckled so hard I thought he was going to choke.

Breaking the barrier? I thought. The thing that separated Imre from the rest of us was that he was not alive. A pretty high barrier.

||||

The crowd erupted in laughter when the Buzzard offence took the field. Imre was literally half the size of the other players. He looked like a doll. His uniform jersey was so big that you couldn't read the number when it was tucked into his pants.

A heavy policeman stood on the sidelines. He was not laughing. "There's that little zombie!" he shouted. "Luther, watch out for the zombie!"

Evil-O grabbed my arm. I recognized the policeman too: Sergeant Sponagle, the meanest man in Dresden. Calvin's dad.

"Why is he here? Crowd control?"

"He's cheering the Cougars. Luther's playing for them this year. Didn't you know? He works in Hope Springs."

"Oh," I said, and then, slower, "Ohh."

Luther Sponagle was older than Calvin, maybe eighteen or nineteen. I'd been hearing about him since kindergarten. Expelled from every school in Dresden for fighting, setting fires, carrying weapons (a pair of pliers, I think, which is not much of a weapon, but that school was already sick of him), and generally being a meanie. He was a great athlete but crazy angry. He got kicked out of one high school for biting his opponent's nose during a wrestling match. Really. He'd be in jail now if his father wasn't a cop. Luther was as mean as sleet. And playing against Imre.

Evil-O is more of a football fan than I am. She could tell you more about the game. All I know is that we didn't do well for most of it. The Cougars had the ball and pushed our guys around. The score was 14–0 with a few minutes left.

And then Imre hit Luther Sponagle and things changed.

Imre hadn't done much up until now. He always seemed to be in the wrong place. One time Evil-O went "Oh no" and covered her eyes. I asked what had happened. She said, "He tackled the wrong guy."

He got it right this time. Our quarterback was running down the field with Imre ahead of him. Luther moved in. *He* had been having a great game until then. Lots of tackles and one of the touchdowns. He didn't try to dodge Imre. I'm sure he figured he could run right over him to get to the quarterback.

He didn't. It was not a head-to-head collision—Imre was too short. More like head-to-stomach. Luther stopped as if he had run into the side of a building, then crumpled at Imre's feet. Our quarterback ran all the way to the goal line. The fans were as surprised as the opposing team—it took a few seconds for the cheers to start.

There was more to cheer about on the very next play—the kickoff. The Cougars were running the kick back. Luther was ahead of the guy with the ball, blocking for him. He launched himself at Imre. I guess he wanted revenge. The way Imre explained it later, it sounded easy.

"Number 57 was flying towards me," he said. "So I caught him out of the air and threw him at those other Cougars, and he knocked them down."

The ref blew his whistle, stopped, and looked at Imre for a second. Then he went to get the ball, shaking his head.

Before the next Cougar play, our number 84—a big lineman—talked to Imre. Then 84 got onto his hands and knees and Imre grabbed him by his belt and shirt. When the play started, Imre *threw* 84 like a bale of hay. He landed on top of the Cougar quarterback, who was so shocked he dropped the ball. Our 84 grabbed it and hung on.

"Foul!" shouted Sergeant Sponagle. "Ref! Ref! Did you see? The zombie cheated! Penalty!"

The game didn't feel like one of our usual losses. We were behind, and there was hardly any time left, but we had the ball and we only needed a touchdown to tie. A lot of us were on our feet. The lady next to me and Evil-O was holding a tiny baby and shouting. She had a high piercing voice, like a teakettle.

"Isn't that little zomboy amazing!" she yelled, jumping up and down.

"Yes, he is!" Evil-O yelled back.

"Yay, Imre!" we shouted together. The baby gurgled happily and then threw up, mostly on my sleeve.

With less than a minute to go, our quarterback did what he should have been doing all day. He simply handed off to Imre and stood aside. Imre moved forward, lifting his legs and putting them down, turning red-shirted Cougars aside like the blade of a snowplow. His jersey was ripped half off, and he had two big linemen on his back and Luther clinging to his ankle when he crossed the goal line. The referee blew his whistle and threw his hands in the air. Touchdown.

The crowd went crazy. "Go Buzzards!" echoed around the field. Part of the green cheering section bent forward, hands outstretched, bowing down to Imre. Johnny panned through the crowd. The photographer from the *Dresden Evening Guide* screwed a giant lens onto her camera.

I didn't care about the baby's spit-up. That's how excited I was. Speaking of excited, Sergeant Sponagle ran right onto the field to yell. The ref pointed to the sidelines, and the sergeant stalked off. When he came to number 57, who was standing with a couple of teammates, he shook his fist at him. "You're pathetic!" I heard him yell at his son, over the noise of the crowd. "Pathetic!"

The score was 14–13 for them, with no time left. Everyone was on their feet.

The teams lined up wrong for the convert. It looked like a regular play.

"Aren't we going to kick?" I asked Evil-O. "Then we'll tie the game."

She shook her head. "Coach is trying for a two-point conversion. If we get the ball into the end zone, we'll win 15–14. Which will be the first time in forever we've beaten the Cougars."

"And if we don't get the ball into the end zone?"

"Then we lose like usual."

Sergeant Sponagle's voice was clear and loud. "Get him!" he shouted. "Get that zombie, you pathetic losers!"

As before, the quarterback took the snap and handed the ball to Imre, who stepped forward into the arms of the entire Cougars team. Imre disappeared under a red tide, but kept moving. The crowd went quiet, like at a tennis match. You could hear the players grunting and swearing. The pile on Imre grew. He was on the two-yard line . . . the one- . . .

Evil-O dug her fingers into my arm.

Imre was carrying or dragging or pushing the entire

Cougars team. It looked like a mountain of laundry moving towards the goal line, wavering, and falling forward.

The ref blew his whistle. The game was over. But had we won? The players got off Imre, who was stretched across the goal line, his arm flung forward and the ball clearly visible. I opened my mouth to cheer, but no words came out. Everyone on the field was frozen, looking at the ball, which lay a couple of feet from Imre. He must have fumbled going over the line.

Or had he? Why hadn't someone grabbed the ball? And then I saw why. Underneath the ball, clearly visible from where I sat, was Imre's hand. Not the rest of him. Just the hand, which was not connected to his arm.

CHAPTER 37

The ref acted as if he had memorized the section of the rule book dealing with body parts under the ball. He blew his whistle, raised his arms over his head, and ruled that the convert was good. The ball had not touched the ground, so there was no fumble. Imre's hand under the ball meant that he was still in possession. No argument, no discussion. Game over. The final score: 15–14 for the Buzzards.

His attitude kept the players calm—even when Imre picked up his unattached hand. The crowd was cheering hard. Not many had actually seen what happened. Most didn't find out the full details until the next day when the *Dresden Evening Guide* ran the story (*Surprise Win! Zomboy Lends a Helping Hand*) on the front page. The photographer's long lens caught a clear image of the ball with Imre's fingers underneath it. You know the shot I mean—you've probably seen it.

We ran onto the field to congratulate Imre, who was his

usual gloomy self. "I hope you enjoyed that last play," he said. "Embarrassment is always more fun when your friends are there to see it."

"You won the game, Imre!" Evil-O looked around. "Is Susan here? I'm so happy I want to rub it in. Remember when she said you couldn't be a team player? Go Buzzards!"

"You pushed those guys around, Imre!" I yelled. "You toasted them! Toasted them brown! Ha ha!"

Next second I wished I hadn't spoken so loud. A group of nearby Cougars turned to glare at us. One of them was Calvin's brother. He came over, wider than a doorway in his shoulder pads. My pulse went from zero to sixty in no time flat.

"What did you say, kid?"

"Nothing!" I said. "I was making a joke. You played great, Luther," I said. "Too bad you didn't win. I mean, I'm a Buzzards fan, but you, uh, you ..."

"You joking about *me*?" He swallowed. "You calling me a piece of *toast*?"

There was spittle at the side of his mouth. He was frothing. I slid around behind Imre. I know it's not cool to use your friends for shelter, but Luther looked mad enough to kill someone, and Imre was already dead.

"Joke? No, no, no! You are not toast. Not even warm. You are very, uh, fresh bread."

With my cold I sounded like Homer Simpson—*d'oh, d'oh, d'oh!* Luther clenched his fists. Evil-O pulled me away and we headed down the sidelines to where Mom and Dad were waiting.

"Idiot," she said.

"I know."

I saw Sergeant Sponagle yelling at Luther, jabbing at him with his finger. That made me feel cold. I saw big number 84 pat Imre on the top of the head. That made me feel warm. I saw a Jeep with a cracked rear window waiting outside the parking lot with the motor running. That made me forget about the football game for a moment, and think about Kato the dog and secrets. Then I went back to worrying about Luther.

"Football is such a violent sport," Mom said on our way home to dinner (spaghetti and meatballs—Dad made the sauce before we left). "Did Imre suffer, poor boy?"

I explained that that kind of thing happened to him all the time. "I'm sure Dr. Bernstein taped his hand back on," I said.

Dad wondered what it would be like to be the trainer on Imre's team. "Better carry lots of tape," he said. "There'd be bits and pieces falling off all the time."

Mom rolled her eyes.

After dinner I blew my nose and washed my hands and felt my forehead. Was I sicker than before? I couldn't tell. I went over to Evil-O's. She and her mom were watching a TV show about the Rocky Mountains. Mrs. Forester really got into the scenery. "Isn't that beautiful, Bob!" she said. "Don't you wish you lived there!"

When a commercial came on she flipped to the cable news channel, which showed pictures of the beach and the water tower and the mayor. The scroll along the bottom gave the time and temperature and local news headlines like this one:

Inter-County Football League: Dresden Buzzards 15, Hope Springs Cougars 14.

"Did Evil-O tell you about the game?" I asked.

"I didn't have to," said Evil-O. "She knew all about it."

Her mom was smiling.

"My boss, Mr. Terwilliger, was there. He called. That little zomboy is a hero! I have to go in to work early tomorrow to arrange a game-themed display. Say, do you two want a snack?"

I blinked. I thought she hated Imre.

Mrs. Forester came back from the kitchen with chocolate Popsicles—my favourite flavour. I thanked her. When she nodded her hair fell across her face, and for a second she looked just like Evil-O. That was weird.

"What's with your mom? Last week she was calling Imre a freak," I said. "Now he's a hero."

We were walking around the block. It was a warm fall evening, smelling like grass and rain. The sky was cloud-covered. Evil-O bit off the end of her Popsicle. Whenever I do that I get a brain freeze but she has no nerves.

"Mr. Terwilliger sold a dozen pairs of black-and-white high-tops before he realized that they were the shoes Imre wears in the bus video. Have you seen the store recently? There's a hundred boxes in the front window and the video is running all the time on a TV right there in the display."

"So Imre is good for business."

"And he'll be even better now because of the football game and the TV show. And if he wins the election."

"Huh. So is your mom proud of you for being crazy and different?"

As soon as I said that I wished I had put it differently. "I mean—"

"I know what you mean, Bob. And no. She still worries that I'll embarrass her somehow. She still—well, she's still her old self. But at least she isn't afraid I'll get her fired tomorrow."

Neither of us said anything for a bit. I listened to the silence, which seemed bigger because of the little sounds— wind in the branches, distant cars, the slurping noises you make eating Popsicles. The street light up ahead was broken. It flickered on and off. The world disappeared and then appeared again as we walked underneath.

"Do you really think I'm crazy, Bob?"

"Noo-oo!" I said, stretching it out and then wishing I hadn't because my voice broke in the middle of the word.

"I mean, of course not," I said.

I wanted to tell her more—how pretty she was, how brave and wonderful, how cool it was to be her friend. I would have told her all this stuff—I was *this* close to telling her— only I felt a huge sneeze coming on and had to press my finger against my upper lip to stop it. And then something whispered along the back of my neck, making me shiver. Were we being followed? I checked over my shoulder.

"Did you feel that, Bob? 'Cause I did too."

A bullfrog cut loose from the pond in the Brownes' front yard. Sounded like a bomb. Evil-O took off. I ran after her.

Pork chops!

CHAPTER 38

Miss Howe rubbed the big 1 off the board. "Ready for the election, class?" she asked. Evil-O turned in her chair with that amazing smile of hers, the one that goes around her face three times. Imre was the most popular kid in the school, maybe in town. Westwood had been lined with people waiting for his bus, cheering and snapping pictures when he got off. He'd been mobbed on the school-yard. Almost everyone had been at the football game, and for those who'd missed it there was already a *Zomboy Touchdown* video on YouTube (with an exclusive link to the CBC). All the way into class, people were after him for auto-graphs. He even signed a few guys' arms. A school hero, all right.

Johnny had filmed the whole thing. He and the rest of the CBC team were at the back of the class now.

Miss Howe handed out empty ballots from a cookie tin.

Susan stood up and said she had an announcement. She looked serious, her hair held back by a white band. Did she have a last-minute surprise for us? She did.

"I am conceding the election," she said. "I don't want to divide the class anymore. Imre has more support than I do. I will withdraw and let him be elected unanimously."

She paused. The look on her face was very hard to read. She turned towards Johnny's camera.

"I do not take back my remarks about Imre. I still think he is a heartless misfit who has no place in a regular school. But he has used his freakish powers to attract you, to appeal to you, to fool you. He and his election team have courted popularity so successfully that I cannot win. I would hate to get only one or two votes, the way my poor opponent did last year—"

"Hey!" said Evil-O.

"—so I will concede now. That is all. Congratulations, President Imre."

Susan sat down. Hands in her lap. Her lips moved as if she was saying grace.

There was a long pause. The camera was rolling. Someone should do something, I thought. When you won, you celebrated, didn't you? Imre was preoccupied and Evil-O was busy glaring at Susan. What should I do? Seconds passed slowly.

Really slowly.

I looked around for inspiration and didn't find any. In fact, I found trouble. My ZOMBOY RULES poster was coming off the wall. The tape at the top gave way, and the cardboard toppled forward. I jumped up and grabbed it just in time.

"Help! Help!" I cried.

But it didn't come out *help*. It came out *hip*. As in *hip hip*. And the class responded.

"Hooray!"

Puzzled, I turned around. I was still holding the poster over my head. Everyone was cheering.

Evil-O gave me the thumbs-up. "Hip! Hip!" she shouted.

"Hooray!" the class shouted back. Now I got it. I marched to the front of the room with the poster held high. Dramatic or what?

"Hip! Hip!"

"Hooray!"

Evil-O started to clap and almost everyone joined in. Susan didn't—she had her lips clamped shut. Calvin didn't either. He had a pretty good black eye. I got one a couple of years ago, slipping on a pile of weasel poop in Evil-O's hall (the weasel was one of Evil-O's help projects—it never did learn to poop in a litter box) and hitting my face on a door-knob. My eye had darkened and flamed for several days, and Calvin's looked like it would do the same. But the rest of the class made a lot of noise. Andrew was whistling through his fingers. I wished I knew how to do that. Gezink was trying to clap his hands over his head, and missing.

I held my pose while the cheering died away. Johnny's camera was on me. And then, with my hands in the air and the class silent and expectant, I exploded.

I was at a hundred and five sneezes by now, over the halfway mark of my cold, and these, the hundred and sixth, seventh, eighth, and ninth, were the biggest sneezes by far—

maybe the biggest of my life. In fact to call them sneezes doesn't do them justice. If a sneeze is a firecracker, these were atom bombs. It was an immense moment, epic, my body bent over, my lungs convulsing, the air around me thick with mucus. I felt as if I was turning inside out, my insides becoming my outsides. When I finished, I was gasping for breath. The class was stunned. Melvin, the director, had both hands on his head, like he was pulling his hair out. Johnny's shoulders were shaking so hard the camera wobbled.

Next period was gym. We went outside to play soccer, reaching the field as a CBC van turned out of the school driveway and headed up the hill. Johnny and the fat man were getting into another van, so Evil-O and Imre and I went over to the parking lot to say goodbye. The fat man's sweater was rust coloured today, with brass buttons. He must have had a whole closet of them. He beamed when he saw us.

"You!" Pointing at Imre. "I've been talking to CNN and the BBC, TF1 in France and RTL in Germany, about the football footage," he said. "The news is great great great. Your face is going to be everywhere!"

"You mean my hand," Imre said gloomily.

"And you!" Pointing at Evil-O. "Melvin and I have talked about you. The camera *loves* you. I'm going to keep your name on file."

"You *are*?" She lit up like a little kid. Then she caught herself. "I mean, you are? That's cool. But, uh, what about Bob?" she asked.

The fat man swung himself sideways into the driver's seat. "Bob?" He started the van. "Bob?" He reached for the door handle. "Bob is—"

The door slammed.

Johnny was beside me with a big grin on his face.

"I guess the camera doesn't *love* me," I said to him. "We're just, you know, friends."

"You. Always with the jokes," he said, slipping into the passenger seat and closing the door. The van roared away.

Last period of the day was our time to share our hobbies. Usually it was Susan tap dancing or Andrew with a math puzzle that nobody but him could do. (Evil-O, who hated hobby share, wanted me to bring in doughnuts—and I would have, only I didn't want to share my hobby with everybody). Anyway, today Gezink brought in a Mega Man action figure. He tried to show us how the left arm became a plasma cannon, only he twisted the wrong way and the hand came off.

"Hey look!" said Calvin, whose eye was eggplant-coloured by then. "Mega Man's like Imre!"

Gezink was upset, but he laughed with the rest of us because what else was he going to do?

"Mega Man's hand isn't supposed to come off," he said.

"Neither is mine," said Imre, gloomily.

CHAPTER 39

WHERE DOES A STORY END?
NOT HERE

Imre's fame didn't die after the football game. There was a skit on *Saturday Night Live* and I was allowed to stay up for it. (Lots of body parts.) They even had a top ten for the advantages to being a zomboy (number four: If you get dealt bad cards you can just throw in your hand). He went to a class presidents' meeting and came back with a poster for the dance. It rained. My cold got better. Ms. Eiger didn't— she picked up another infection in the hospital. Gezink got a new pair of glasses that made him look like a deep-sea diver. Mrs. Berdit finally stopped protesting. Mom had a giant tolerance party at our place. (Did they drink wine and give each other high-fives? Did they link arms and sing "If I Had a Hammer"? Did I run upstairs and hide?) It kept raining. Me and Evil-O sat under an umbrella to watch the Buzzards lose to the Castleton Dragons. Imre wasn't there. The league wouldn't let him play if he was going to lose body parts.

That was the day before the Halloween dance. That evening the rain finally stopped. Evil-O got out her skateboard and I took my bike and we cruised up around the mall. She wanted to keep going, to Imre's place. He hadn't been at school that day and she wanted to see how he was doing.

"Maybe he's really sick," she said.

"How can he be?" I asked.

"Well, there's something going on with him, don't you think?"

"No way." I still hadn't told her about Kato. "I mean, uh, maybe. Yeah, now that I think about it, maybe you're right. Or maybe not. But if there is something going on I don't know about it."

I am so bad at secrets.

On our way home from the mall, Mrs. Good nearly ran us off the road. She rolled down her window and asked if we'd seen Razor. We shook our heads.

"He must have got loose again. You sure you haven't seen him?"

"Sorry," I said. Not meaning it.

"You kids are useless!" She roared away.

No more talk about Imre. With Razor on the loose, we hurried home. Mom was in the kitchen with the computer turned on, watching Rappin' ZED's new video. Mrs. Stinson wore white makeup with a pretend scar on her face. The sign she held said I ♥ ZOMBOY.

||||

Give a holler for tolerance
Stand taller, don't fall or
Be left behind, no axe to grind.
Got the means to shine
In your new state of mind,
Pass it on, sister
Can't resist
The distance from A to B,
You to me,
New to old, hot to cold,
Living, dying,
Demystifying, the truth
Shall set you free, sea to sea,
Free to look in the book where the word is,
Not the bush where the bird is,
Two there, one in your hand,
What's your plan?
What it's worth, across the earth?
Tolerance.

CHAPTER 40

Thursday the 24th, the day of the Halloween dance, was a late summer leftover, sunny and almost warm enough for me to think about short sleeves before deciding on a sweatshirt. There was a PA day the next day, which made this the last morning of the school week. Who was complaining? Not me.

Evil-O's mom came to the front door with her.

"Did you get your lunch? I put in chocolate chip cookies."

"Thanks, Mom. Bye."

"Bye, Olive backwards."

I had never heard her call her that before. Olive backwards was Evil-O. Come to think of it, I couldn't remember the last time Evil-O's mom had made her lunch.

The maples and oaks on the way to school were all kinds of orange and red, and whatever tree that is on Mrs. Dithyramb's front lawn was an amazing pure yellow. Evil-O kicked and rolled down the leaf-scattered sidewalk. I walked beside her, watching her hair bounce up and down on her neck. It was one of those mornings that made you feel good to be alive. I didn't know who I should be thanking, but I was grateful for it. Until I heard Imre's news, that is.

"You're *moving*?" I said. "Where to?"

He didn't know. Somewhere north, he thought. We were standing by our lockers. Kids streamed past us on their way to class.

"When is the move?"

"This weekend."

"Wow," I said. "That's fast." I stared down at his raccoon eyes in his pasty broken face. "Do you want to move?"

"No!" He said it loud enough to turn heads. "No. But Dr. Bernstein says we have to."

"Because of—Kato." I whispered the last word.

"She's getting worse. Dr. Miller found her on the road last night. She escaped again. They talk about her all the time. They're worried about her. She had to have extra tests yesterday. Me too."

His usual gloom was kind of funny, but not this time. I thought about him—how weird and mysterious he was, and also how decent. How he never got angry or said anything mean. How much Evil-O liked him. How much I did. I thought, I'm going to miss him.

Huh.

I also thought, now Susan will get to be class president. But I seemed to care less about that than I did about Imre.

"So you're moving because your dog is sick?" I said.

"What?"

"Kato is a dog, right? Or is she some other kind of animal?"

"What are you talking about, Bob? You saw her."

I pictured the moving bundle in Dr. Miller's arms, heard the growls.

"I thought you knew about her," he said. "You're so smart and all. And you promised not to tell."

He sighed. It was like he *wanted* someone to know about Kato. Someone to share her with.

"She's my sister," he said.

"What?"

"My baby sister. Kato is her name. It is short for Katalin."

"What!?"

"Shh."

Evil-O came over with her books piled on her head, practising her balance. "Great to see you back at school, Imre. I was worried about you."

"Thank you, Evil-O."

"What's up? You guys look all serious."

"Nothing," said Imre quickly. "Nothing at all. Bob and I were talking about the dance tonight."

"Wait till you see Bob dance, he's hilarious."

And with her back straight, arms slightly out from her body, the books teetering, Evil-O glided past us.

"Why not take your—Kato to a hospital?" I whispered. "That's what normally happens when someone is sick."

"We're *not* normal, Bob. We can't go to a town hospital. Anyway, Dr. Bernstein is afraid I'll get sick too."

I wondered what he meant. He was already dead—what could happen to him? What would Dr. Bernstein say? *This flu of yours is getting very serious, Imre. If we don't treat it you might even . . . oh, no, wait. You already are.*

I couldn't pay attention in math class, and it wasn't because number lines were hard. Kato was a girl! Imre wasn't the only one rescued from the nuclear disaster. He had a baby sister. That's who the high chair in the kitchen was for. I wondered if the army's plan was for her to come to kindergarten when she was old enough. I wondered what was wrong with her.

Miss Howe was looking hopefully at me.

"Sorry, what was the question?"

"Do you want to tell us what negative five plus negative thirteen is, Bob?"

"No," I said without having to think about it. "No, I don't."

We played tag during last recess. Evil-O chased Imre to the very top of the climber, way above where she and I had jumped to our doom on the first day of school. Imre didn't jump—he leaned back and let himself go, falling flat onto the gravel. Evil-O slithered down a level and ran after Gezink, whose new glasses had fallen off. He called time-out to grope around for them. Gezink was always taking time-outs.

A crowd of smaller kids came over to see if Imre was okay. He sat up, dusting himself off. He said he was fine. "That was so cool, when you fell!" they cried. Their high-pitched voices sounded like birds calling. *So cool. So cool.*

CHAPTER 41

That evening was the scariest of my life by far. I'm still getting over it. The dance was for grades six and seven only. The gym was decorated with black and orange streamers and fake spiderwebs. A cardboard—not candy— skeleton dangled from the clock in the middle of the wall. Mr. Buzminski was onstage, being the DJ. Swarty poured me a glass of punch and made a joke about my pirate costume not fitting.

"It's the same one as last year," I said.

"Mine too." She was a rabbit. "But I'm the same size. You've grown."

The disco ball hanging from the front of the stage sent scraps and patches of light around the gym. I drank my punch and moved onto the dance floor, wiggling my arms and bending, letting my mind whirl along with the ball. Evil-O makes fun of me but I can't help it—I get carried away by the music. I thought about everyone cheering when Imre got up onstage as the president of the senior class to open the dance. I thought how great it was not to have a camera beside me. I thought about costumes: Did they say who you were? If so, then Evil-O was a ninja warrior with a bow and arrow and tight-fitting hood. Swarty was a rabbit, Mr. Dejardin a burglar, Dakota and Debbie princesses in long gowns and crowns, Gezink a bunch of grapes, and I was a pirate in too-tight pants.

I couldn't see very well, what with the lighting and my eye patch, and I bumped into Debbie and got hissed at. Then I bumped into Gezink and popped one of his purple balloons.

Someone elbowed me in the ribs. I turned and there was Calvin Sponagle, breathing heavily, fists clenched.

"Really?" I said. "Are you going to go *pow!* in the middle of the dance floor?"

"Shut up, Bob. Where's Imre?"

"I don't know. He's in a sailor costume."

Which was funny since half the dance was dressed like zomboys. Imre wore white bellbottoms and a sailor shirt and one of those silly round hats. He said he'd found the outfit in the basement of his house.

Calvin had gone home at lunch and hadn't come back during the school day. He didn't have a costume. His skin was slick with sweat and his shoulders trembled.

"I came to warn Imre," he said, with pauses to breathe. "It's serious."

⦀

We met in the change room: me and Imre and Calvin and Evil-O. No one said anything about Evil-O being in the boys' room.

"You all know about my brother, Luther," said Calvin.

"You mean he's weird and mean? Yeah," said Evil-O.

Calvin gave a sick little laugh. "Ever since that football game with the Buzzards he's been stranger than normal. No one can handle him, not even my dad. He gave me a black eye 'cause he thought I was you, Imre. That's what he said anyway . . . 'You zombie,' he said and—*whack*. He talks about you all the time. He's playing bad and he blames you. Says you turned him into toast. I don't know where he got that idea but he goes on and on about it. 'I'm not toast,' he says. 'Not a piece of toast.'"

Evil-O and I looked at each other.

"I'm lying on the couch tonight," said Calvin, "feeling like crap and wishing the apartment was warmer, when Luther comes in with RJ from the garage. RJ says tonight's the night 'cause his mom's back and he can get her car. The two of them're going over to your place, Imre. I heard them planning it out. They were going to go last week but RJ's mom went on vacation and Luther had games out of town. It was creepy listening to them work themselves up. They just want to bash zombies. They didn't know I was there 'cause I was at the other end of the room, under sheets and blankets. Soon as they left, I headed up here."

"Why?" I asked.

Calvin ignored me. "Luther and RJ do crazy stuff. They wreck things. That fire at the Dairy Queen—that was them.

And all those windows smashed on King Street last week. Luther told me about it. He was laughing."

Through the walls I could hear the beat of the song. Not the notes, just the bass.

"Thanks, Calvin," said Evil-O. "But Imre's place is safe. How does your creepy brother think he's going to get past the fence and the soldiers? The house is guarded, right Imre?"

"Not anymore," he said slowly. "The army is still on call. Dr. Bernstein checks in with Colonel Chipelski. But there are no guards there now."

"Aren't you guys worried about reporters?"

"They have not been around for a while." Imre shrugged. "Zombies are not news unless we're lifting buses or winning football games."

"Well, geez!" Evil-O jumped to her feet. Instant-action girl. "We have to do something. You don't have a phone, do you? Let's borrow Swarty's so you can call home. Come on!"

She ran out of the room, pulling Imre after her.

Calvin sat on a bench, breathing through his open mouth. His eyes were glazed.

He was sick, all right. I made sure to stay away from him. But I really wanted to know.

"Why are you doing this, Calvin?"

"This—"

"Dragging yourself over here to warn Imre. You hate him. What's going on?"

Calvin shook his head and muttered something about Susan Berdit.

196

"What?"

"Remember the football game? We're sitting together at the back and Susan turns to me and do you know what she says? She says, 'I'm ashamed of myself.' Is that wacky?"

"Yes," I said. "Yes, that is wacky."

"Her mom is yelling at Susan to beat Imre and win the election, and Susan can't stand it. I hate Susan, but the thing is, I know how she feels."

His head hung. A drop of sweat formed on the end of his nose and dripped onto the concrete floor of the change room.

"You're ashamed too. I get it. For calling Imre names and picking on me, eh?"

He looked up. "What do you mean, picking on you? You're a loser, Bob. A super-loser."

"Right. Right. Sorry. I knew that. So, uh, about Imre, then?"

"The guy's a zombie, but he's okay. I don't hate him. I don't . . ." His voice trailed off. He shook his head.

I was aware of how unlikely this moment was. Calvin was sick, saying things he would not normally say to anyone. We were never going to be close like this again.

"Who *do* you hate, Calvin?"

"Luther." He thought a minute, like he was going to add something, another name. I waited. He didn't say anything else.

Evil-O poked her head in. The black ninja hood kept her hair in, made her eyes look bigger. "No answer," she said. "Imre wants to go home right now. He's worried."

About Kato, I knew. His little sister, who was sick.

"What about the police?" I asked.

"My dad isn't going to let anyone help Imre. He'd probably help Luther tear his head off." Calvin laughed harshly and drew a painful breath. "After that football game, I thought my dad was going to explode."

I noticed that Calvin never called his father *Dad*. It was always, *my dad*. Like he was trying to connect himself to his father.

What a mess the Sponagles were.

"Bob, come on!" said Evil-O.

I stood up. Imre's secret was a bond between us. I knew something about him that no one else did. Also, I was the one who had called Luther a piece of toast, so I was partly responsible for driving him crazy. Crazier. And Evil-O was my best friend. Yeah, I was in this up to my ears.

Calvin sat forward on the bench with his elbows on his knees and the sweat dripping off his face.

"You know, you're not a totally bad guy," I said.

He didn't move or say anything, and I left.

CHAPTER 42

I caught up with Imre and Evil-O at the bike rack. Imre was bent over, breaking the locks of the three nearest machines. I said nothing. In an emergency, all the rules go overboard. We could return the bikes later. We headed up Westwood to Elgin and along to where it turned into Highway 2, three of us in a line, sailor, ninja, pirate. Imre had to stretch to reach the pedals, but he was going fast. I guess you never do forget how to ride a bike—not even when you're dead. Evil-O's legs pumped like pistons. I was falling behind. I gave an extra push and felt my pants rip.

The mall clock was flashing 8:30 when we passed. The wind sang in the overhead wires. It was a long long *long* way to Furillo Family Farms. It takes two minutes to drive there, but space is bigger on a bike. I felt like an ant walking across a picnic blanket.

There was a floodlight on a pole halfway down Imre's lane. That was it for lighting. It got too muddy to ride, so we got off our bikes. The sound of my ragged breathing matched the whooshing of the wind. No, wait, that wasn't wind. I looked around.

"D'you hear *buzzing*?" I asked.

It was coming from under the light pole. There was a cloud of night bugs around some roadkill. Too big for a raccoon.

"Oh, yes," said Imre. "That dog."

"Dog?"

"You remember him, Bob. He attacked you. Dr. Miller found his body last night."

Sure enough, it was Razor. Evil-O and I stared at the familiar black-and-brown body. Razor, no longer the terror of the neighbourhood.

"He must have been hit by a car," I said. "Remember what Mrs. Good told us last night, Evil-O? He must have got run over and wandered up this lane to die."

"With his head off?"

Evil-O was closer than I was. She kicked at Razor, and his head came away from his body and rolled a little way. I did not let out a scream.

"Quiet, Bob! You are such a girl."

All right, maybe a little scream.

Imre's place was even spookier at night. The weather vane clanged away on the roof. Light streamed out onto the porch through the front windows and the big door, which closed with a *bang* and then blew open again. Imre ran up the steps, sailor shirt flapping in the wind. His hat was gone. Evil-O and I followed. I don't know if she stuck close to me or the other way around.

Imre was shouting. I'd never heard him shout before.

"Who's Kato?" Evil-O asked me.

"His sister."

"He has a *sister*?"

"It's a secret. She's sick, and getting sicker. That's why they have to move."

"They're moving? Geez!"

There was a strong smell of gasoline. I heard Evil-O sniff—she'd caught it too. We checked the hall and the living room to the right of the hall. We didn't see anyone. The front door banged behind us.

"How do you know so much, Bob?"

"Imre told me."

"And when did you learn to keep a secret?"

"I—"

"I mean really. I thought we were friends!"

With her black ninja hood up hiding her hair, and her eyes flashing with interest, anger, and fear she was beautiful. The things you think of.

There were dark stains on the kitchen floor, drips and blotches. They led towards the back of the house. A butcher-shop smell mixed with the gasoline.

My throat tightened. Could the stains be blood? If they were, how did they get there? Luther? Was he still here?

"Kato?" yelled Imre. "Kato, where are you? Come out. It's me!"

I wanted to run out the front door and keep going until I got to Mexico.

A hockey helmet with a cage front lay on the floor by the high chair. I didn't understand. Evil-O was fiddling with the telephone.

"No dial tone," she said. "The wind must have knocked down the line."

We followed the stains through the kitchen. The door at the back led to an office. When I got to the doorway all I saw was Dr. Bernstein's body lying in a pool of blood. He was on the floor beside the long desk. The blood was under and around him, mostly by his legs and feet. His face was as white as milk, except for his dark eyes and thick glasses. He was alive, though. His eyes flickered.

"We have to get you to the hospital!" said Evil-O. "Do you have a cell phone? Bob, look around—"

"No," the doctor interrupted. "You cannot save my life. Or any of the others'. The experiment has failed. Again. The army is coming. They will be too late. Typical." It was hard for him to talk. He had to keep taking breaths. "Imre, stay here. Girl and boy. You must go. Go now!"

Where does certainty come from? Bits of information came together in my mind like puzzle pieces. The hockey helmet. The high chair with blood on it. Dr. Miller's gloves. The hole under the fence. The dead animals.

This horror wasn't about Luther.

"It's Kato," I said to the doctor. "Kato bit you, didn't she."

He let out a long sigh.

"Damn it, Imre," I said. "You should have told us!"

But he had left the room. It was just Evil-O and me now.

"What is it, Bob?" she said. "What should he have told us?"

"Kato is a zom*bie*. Not a zom*boy* like Imre. She's the kind you see in movies and video games. She's a *real* zombie."

The wind was howling. Tree branches banged against the side of the house.

"Right, Dr. Bernstein?" I said. "That's her sickness—she's a zombie. She wears a hockey helmet so she won't attack people or animals. Too bad she learned how to take it off."

He took another long sighing breath.

"Animals?" Evil-O gaped. "You mean *Razor*?"

"And those chickens of Mrs. Furillo's. They thought it was a coyote but it wasn't. Kato escapes sometimes. Remember the hole by the fence? Imre says she likes to hide, and dig under things. They're worried about her, and that's why they're moving."

I could hear Imre upstairs, calling out.

"There were two survivors from Fort Sterling," I said. "A zomboy and his zombie sister. That's what this experiment is about. There must be two kinds of that *pedes mortuus* thing. The army wants to know what makes Imre different. Or what makes Kato different from Imre. It was secret, which is why they didn't want the CBC filming here. Now it's a giant mess and they have to move and *we have to go*!"

Evil-O was frowning, working it out. I grabbed her arm and pulled.

"Hurry!" I said. "He could turn into a zombie too!"

The doctor's head had fallen forward on his chest. Was he dead or sleeping or getting ready to transform? And he wasn't the only thing to worry about. There were the downed phone lines, the open front door, the smell of gasoline. Who knew where Kato was? I checked over my shoulder, expecting to see a zombie *right behind me* the way it works in the movies. But there was no one there.

I felt like I had swallowed a bomb. I was *this close* to my nightmare.

"Wait!" Evil-O said. "I have to say goodbye. How much time do we have?"

I hate to play boys versus girls. Evil-O is nothing like Dakota or Susan, or my mom or Grandma. But right then, when she asked how much time we had, I thought, what a *girl* thing to say. If you tell a guy to hurry because there are zombies around, the guy will not ask questions. He will hurry. Even Gezink would hurry.

Girls will drive you crazy sometimes. They just will.

"I don't *know* how much time we have!" I may have shouted. "Maybe hours, maybe minutes. This isn't a movie. What does it matter how much time we have? Kato is somewhere around here right now. Come *on!*"

I pulled Evil-O through the kitchen and living room and stopped dead. Standing in the hall, between us and the door, was Luther Sponagle. He was wearing half of an orange T-shirt. The other half had been ripped off him. I could see his flat stomach and the muscles of one arm. His exposed flesh was criss-crossed with streaks of blood and at least one bite mark. He pointed at me and made a growling sound.

Is anything faster than thought? In a flash I knew that Luther had been here long enough to be bitten and infected by Kato. He was a zombie. In the same flash, I recognized the plastic canister in his hand as the source of the gasoline smell, heard Imre from upstairs telling me to watch out, and felt Evil-O pulling me backwards towards the kitchen. All this was instantaneous and crystal clear. From then on, my memory of events is a little hazy.

CHAPTER 43

Seeing Luther, I wasn't *more* scared than before. You can only fill a bathtub to the top.

Evil-O ran through the kitchen and up the narrow back staircase. I started after her, slipped on the blood and went down hard, banging the back of my head on the floor. Bells rang, but not for school. I was dizzy, and I stayed dizzy for the rest of the night. Everything I remember from then on flickers around the edges like an old movie. Maybe that's a good thing.

I scrambled after Evil-O but went the wrong way, down to the basement. The lighting was dim. I ducked behind a counter and tried to take my pulse, but I couldn't keep count. A raindrop landed on my hand. And another. That didn't make sense. I stared down. The drops were red. There was blood dripping off the edge of the counter. Blood on the floor too. I looked over my shoulder and saw two zombies crawling towards me. Dr. Miller's left index finger was missing. That was where the blood had come from. One of her eyes was missing too. The other was a blank grey ball bearing. Beside her was a weasely guy with a ripped shirt and blood running down his arm. He was making weird jerky motions. He wasn't crawling very well. This would be Luther's friend RJ.

I staggered away from them. The basement was set up like a hospital room, with a bed and a bunch of machines. Over the bed was a glass cabinet with a pistol inside and a sign that said TRANQUILIZER DART. I fumbled open the cabinet and took down the gun.

The place reeked of gasoline. There was a can lying on its side on the floor. RJ must have dropped it.

Dr. Miller lurched to her feet. I raised the pistol, pulled the trigger. Nothing happened. Crap. I took a step back, and heard someone calling my name, the way you hear your name in a dream. *Bob, Bob, Bob.* Evil-O was beckoning from the top of the basement stairs. I floated up to her. I told her it was great to see her.

"Are you okay?" she whispered.

"I'm fine!" I sat beside her on the top step. The kitchen was behind us, empty.

"Shh."

"There's zombies down there," I said. "Dr. Miller and RJ. She bit him, so he's a zombie now. Do you smell the gas?" I yawned. "Hey, it's great to see you, Evil-O. Where's Imre?"

"You've got to whisper, Bob. Everyone's after us. Luther is upstairs. I don't know where Dr. Bernstein is. Let's just find Imre and get out of here."

"It's like hide-and-seek, you know? They're hiding and we're seeking. No, wait. They're seeking and we're—"

"Shut up, Bob."

"Ollie ollie out are in free."

"Shut up! What is wrong with you? Here, give me that."

I was waving the pistol around. She took it from me.

"A dart gun? Fantastic!"

She pulled a lever at the side and the gun gave a *click*. Now it was ready to fire, she said, but there was only one dart, so we had to make it count. I told her again how happy I was to see her, and she told me to shut up. We went to the front hall. Dr. Bernstein was standing by the door. He had the look. He lurched towards us. I heard noises behind me in the kitchen so I knew we couldn't go there. Evil-O pushed me upstairs, whispering to me to go quietly.

The next bit is totally mixed up in my memory. I don't know if it was five minutes or an hour. I get flashes but not in any kind of order. I wasn't scared then. I'm more scared now, thinking back. At the time it was a game, a cartoon chase with Evil-O and Imre and me running from room to room, one step ahead of the bad guys.

Imre—what a mistake that was! We were creeping up the back stairs when a figure appeared in the doorway above us. I grabbed the gun from Evil-O and fired in one motion. The dart hit Imre in the chest. I hadn't recognized him in time. He crumpled sideways. When we got to him he was fast asleep. The hallway was empty. Evil-O looked like she was about to clonk me.

"*One* single shot," she hissed. "We had *one* chance with this thing, and you shot the *only* person in this house we *don't* have to be scared of!"

Put like that, it sounded kind of funny. But I knew she was right to be mad. I said I was sorry.

"We can't leave him for Luther," she said.

I agreed. So I took Imre's shoulders and Evil-O took his feet, and we carried him between us as we played hide-and-seek through the house.

CHAPTER 44

Flash: Dr. Miller shuffled down the long upstairs hall. We ducked into a bathroom, wondering if she'd seen us. A moment later the door handle rattled, and I spoke without thinking.

"Give me a minute!" I called. "Almost done."

Evil-O glared at me. The door smashed open. Dr. Miller lurched forward. Fortunately, the bathroom had a second door leading to the bedroom beside it. We escaped that way.

Flash: Three of us hiding under a double bed. Zombies outside in the hall, bumping into things. Imre started to snore loudly. Evil-O reached up, grabbed a pillow from the bed, and stuck it over his mouth. I whispered that we didn't want to suffocate him, then realized how silly that was. I started to laugh. Evil-O elbowed me in the side.

✚✚✚

Flash: We were in the office at the back of the house, hiding in the big closet. Dr. Bernstein was gone, but the smell of blood was very strong. I heard a low coughing growl, the sound a dog might make. I recognized it right away.

She spoke. "Eat," she said. At least that's what it sounded like. "Eat!" That's my only memory of Kato during this running-around time.

Flash: Kneeling halfway up the front stairs, peering over the banister into the hall. Luther, RJ, Dr. Miller, and Dr. Bernstein were down there in a group. They swayed and groaned. Blood spatter was all over their clothes. Luther held his head at an odd angle, like his neck was broken. The wind made the windows rattle. RJ's shirt hung off one shoulder and he was fumbling something out of the front pocket. It took forever. When he finally got it, he held it up, squinting, like he was trying to remember what it was for. A small shiny something. Evil-O swore, and dragged me the rest of the way upstairs.

Flash: We were in a creepy nursery. The crib was made of metal, with manacles attached to the four corners. Next to it was a cage—really, a cage with bars, like for a very large dog. The ceiling light was caged too. The table in the corner had medical instruments on it—needles and things. If Hannibal Lecter was a baby, this is where you'd put him.

"Kato's room," I whispered.

We put Imre down. Evil-O slumped to the floor. I went over to the window. The wind was going crazy. The tree branch outside was bouncing up and down. Clouds were racing across the sky and you could see bits of moon. An idea was floating around in my head but I couldn't grab it. It had to do with the bars on the window.

I turned back and found that Evil-O was crying. I had never seen her cry, not even when she tore her hand on the top of a barbed-wire fence a few years ago, and had to go to the hospital for stitches. We had walked home together, her with her hands cupped to hold the blood, swearing constantly. I was the one with tears on my cheeks. When we got to the emergency room, I fainted.

I didn't know what to do now. I stared carefully at a corner of the ceiling and thought about food.

"Sorry, Bob," she said after a moment.

"No problem."

"It's just . . . I can't . . ."

"Yeah."

"They're all zombies, aren't they," she said. "How did that happen?"

"Kato bit the woman doctor—her finger. I saw it. And Luther and RJ got in and Kato bit them. Or maybe the doctor did."

"They're all chasing us and the place is full of gasoline and what's his name has a lighter. Did you see it? He was trying to light it."

"Luther and RJ set fires. Or, they used to. Calvin told me. That must be why they brought the gasoline. They wanted to get back at Imre for making Luther lose that football game. They were going to set this place on fire."

We were sitting on the floor, leaning against the wall with our feet out in front of us. Evil-O's legs were long and thin in their black costume. One of her ninja slippers had a hole in the toe. My pirate pants were filthy, tattered. I put my arm around her. Mushy, I know, but what the heck. I jiggled her a bit to make her feel better.

"What are we going to do, Bob? We have to get out. But I can't think how."

"Maybe you'll get an idea," I said.

"Oh, Bob."

"Or I will."

We had got up again and were carrying Imre when, outside Imre's bedroom, he slipped out of my hands. I was trying to hold on to his legs and they flopped out of my grasp. His door was open and the moon shone in through his window, lighting up the whole room. I saw the chair he and I had spun around in a million years ago. And, through the window, I saw the tree.

And there was an idea.

We dragged him into the room and shut the door. The nearest branch was only a step away from the window. It was thick and angled slightly down to the trunk. You could slide or wriggle along it and then climb down to the front lawn. Evil-O was worried about Imre. We couldn't leave him, we couldn't climb down with him, and he couldn't get down on his own. I had an answer.

"Remember how he dropped off the top of the climber, playing tag?" I said. "This is only a bit higher."

So we sat him on the windowsill, and Evil-O said, "One, two, three," and we pushed him out. He half turned over in the air, landed on his back on the grass, bounced once, and lay still.

"See?" I said.

Then it was our turn. I went first. It was a wobbly journey with the wind tossing the tree around, but I didn't stop to worry about it. I was happy to be out of that house, and I was still kind of loopy inside. I scraped my hands and my pants ripped some more and I could not have cared less. Evil-O was right behind me.

We were in the yard. We were alone. We were safe.

She was smiling for the first time in a while. "You look ridiculous in that costume, Bob. I've been meaning to say it all night."

"Oh."

Her smile grew, and she stepped towards me, and for a second I thought she was going to give me a hug, but she stopped short and put a hand on my arm. "You—" she began.

Just then a small body rose out of the earth and launched itself at her, growling. Arms and legs spread, oversized head with curls blowing in the wind, the baby latched onto the back of her leg, knocking her over. Kato! The front door was open and she had got out. *She likes to dig,* Imre had said. I grabbed at her and we all ended up on the wet muddy overgrown grass together. When Kato threw back her head, I saw the bloodstains black in the moonlight, the shadowy gaps between the little baby teeth.

"Eat," she said, in her deep growl.

My world was falling apart right here, right now, just when I had thought we were safe. Evil-O would turn into a zombie. She would lurch and drool and not be my friend. I couldn't let it happen. Couldn't. I found a tree branch in the grass and jammed it into Kato's mouth. Her little jaws opened wide and she bit and held on. Oh, she was strong! She grabbed Evil-O's arm and twisted. Evil-O screamed. We rolled around for what seemed like a long time. Lights flashed in front of my eyes. It was awful. Maybe the awfullest part of the whole awful day. When I felt someone grab my shoulders, and smelled a science experiment right next to me, I was sure that the other zombies had got out somehow. But when I rolled over to face the new threat, it turned out to be Imre, and he was smiling.

He held his sister tightly.

"There you are, Kato!" he was saying, with his face next to hers. "I was worried about you."

She had her legs wrapped around his waist and was hugging him and butting him with her head.

"Eat," she said.

He held out a finger and she worried at it.

Evil-O was sitting up, cradling her arm. "You okay, Bob? Did she get you?"

"No. You?"

"No."

"That's good. That's ... great."

Her hood was down and her hair stuck out. She struggled to her feet, taking huge breaths. Her left arm was bent at an unnatural angle. She had her mouth clamped firmly. She took a step and collapsed into my arms.

216

Imre went over to a shed at the far end of the property and returned with a backpack, some cans of dog food, and another hockey helmet. He loaded the dog food into the side pockets of the backpack, except for one can, which he popped open. Kato lunged at it.

"You're running away," I said.

Imre had the backpack open on the grass, and was sliding baby Kato into it while she made a mess of eating the dog food. He put the football helmet on her and snapped it in place. Then he swung the pack onto his shoulders. Kato fit pretty well, with only the helmet sticking out.

"You've thought about this," I said. "You planned it."

"People do not understand Kato," he said. "She is not mean or violent, usually. But she did not like what Dr. Miller and Dr. Bernstein were doing to her. She hates the experiments. I cannot let the army have her again."

"But—" I began.

"Ridiculous, isn't it? A zombie with feelings. But I worry about her."

I know you do," I said. "But—"

"You may not believe a zombie can care."

"It's not that," I said. "But your sister is, well, dangerous. She almost got Evil-O."

"That is why I want to be with her. I can keep others from her and her from others. I am strong enough to deal with her. I hope I can do a better job without other people interfering."

He sighed—big brother with a troubled sister. You carry your family around with you, don't you? Good thing Imre was so strong.

Kato was trying to feed herself, making little growling sounds and poking her fingers through the mask.

"Where will you go?" I asked.

He shrugged. "I will keep walking in one direction and see what happens. Wherever we are, Kato and I, we will be together."

"It won't be much fun. The army will be looking for you."

"You like fun, don't you, Bob?"

"I'll *miss* you," I said.

He nodded. "I'll miss you too. You and Evil-O."

She was lying on the grass, breathing evenly.

"Will you help the army find me, Bob?"

I put out my hands. "How could I help them? I won't know where you are. And anyway you're my friend, Imre. I'm not telling."

He gave one of his brief, rare smiles.

"Thank you, Bob."

The wind had been dying down but now it kicked up one more time in a thunderous gust. For five seconds, ten, fifteen, speech was impossible. Towards the end of this last big blow there was a sound like a *crack* from the world's largest whip. The tree we had just climbed down split in half near the base of the trunk. A hundred feet of rotten old wood fell to the ground, bringing down power lines in a shower of sparks. The lights in the house went out, but I caught a flicker of flame near the steps as the sparks lit the gallons and gallons of gasoline. Fire spread like gossip and in half a minute the whole front of the house was blazing.

My last sight of Imre was him trudging into a cornfield

heading away from Dresden. Hope Springs was that way, then Bowville, Oswego, Higginston, Toronto. I wondered if he'd be able to keep himself and his sister hidden or if there'd be more zombie headlines. He loved Kato a lot and she loved him back. If anyone could keep her quiet, it'd be him. I wondered if I'd ever hear from him again. I'd have to keep checking YouTube for *Zomboy Juggles Motorcycles* or something.

The fire was growing. Flames licked up the sides of the house now. The place was made of wood and soaked in gasoline. It would burn to the ground. There'd be nothing left.

I tried to pick up Evil-O. She was awkward to carry and I ended up dragging her along. Halfway down the muddy lane, I saw the back end of a car mostly hidden by a bush. Probably RJ's—the one he and Luther had come in. I wondered if Calvin would miss his brother at all. Sure he hated him, but *never again* is a long time. The fire crackled and roared behind us. I wondered about getting Evil-O to the hospital. I was very tired.

The helicopter swooped low, circling over our heads. I could hear it clearly over the fire. A searchlight shone at us. The machine landed in the field behind the Furillos' place and a squad of soldiers ran over, waving pistols and shouting for me to stop. I did. They asked where we came from. When I pointed back at the burning house, they shot me. I remember staring down at a dart sticking out of my chest. It was the same kind as the one I'd shot Imre with.

CHAPTER 45

I woke up in a bed, with a headache. Boring green walls, bright lights, machines going *bloop* and *bleep* and a clock on the wall that said 03:10. Two beds in the room. Evil-O was in the other one, glaring at a tall doctor.

"I'm not dyslexic," she said. "It's how I say my name."

"Sorry, sorry," he said. "Evil-O Forester. May 21st. Beattie Crescent."

He had red hair and freckles. And a clipboard.

"And how many fingers am I holding up now, uh, Evil-O?"

"Same as last time," she said.

"Say the number, please. For the record. How many fingers?"

"Eleven."

She turned away. She was wearing a hospital gown. Her left arm was in a bright new plaster cast.

When he saw I was awake, he introduced himself as Dr. Owen. He explained that we were in an army hospital in

221

Trent. He took my pulse and temperature, and gave me the same routine as Evil-O. Name, birthday, address, fingers.

"Three," I said.

"Good." He wrote it down. "And how does your head feel?"

"It hurts."

"How much?"

"A lot."

"On a scale of zero to ten, zero meaning no pain and ten meaning high pain, how much does your head hurt?"

I blinked up at him. "What?"

He said it again.

I looked over at Evil-O. "It's a number line, isn't it?"

She nodded.

"We have them in math," I said to the doctor. "I'm no good at them."

We told him our story, all we could remember, how we had ridden over to Imre's from the school dance and found the place full of zombies.

"What zombies?" said the doctor.

We tried to piece the rest of the evening together. It didn't sound very sensible, the two of us carrying Imre upstairs and downstairs, playing hide-and-seek.

"It's hard to remember the order things happened in," I said.

Dr. Owen said he understood. He apologized for the army shooting me. They were under pressure, he said. The helicopter had been delayed by the windstorm. The soldiers panicked when they saw us. "But you guys did well," he said. "You survived an army emergency even though you were wounded. We're treating you as heroes."

We wanted to know about the zombies. "Did they all get burned?" asked Evil-O. "Was there anything left?"

"Zombies?" said the doctor. "What zombies?"

He shone a flashlight into my eyes and made me wince. He apologized for that too. He seemed like a nice enough guy.

"So what happens now?" asked Evil-O.

"Colonel Chipelski wants to talk to you. You'll be going home soon, though. Your parents are here."

He left us alone.

"So, 03:30, that's in the morning, right? Wow, it's late. I'm starved."

She gave me a crooked *aw shucks* kind of smile.

"Did you carry me away from the house, Bob?"

"Uh, kind of. There was some carrying."

"They said you were carrying me." She lowered her voice. "What about Imre? Is he okay? And his—"

"I don't know where he is, but he's safe. I think."

"And his little sister?"

"He took Kato with him. "

I had a sudden picture of the two of them in a forest somewhere, being attacked by a cougar. I knew who I would put my money on. I had no idea how they were going to live— but on the other hand, they weren't really living anyway so maybe that didn't matter so much.

Evil-O shuddered. "What are we supposed to say about them?" she whispered.

"Dunno. Nothing?"

Our beds were close together. I reached over to touch her cast. It went from her hand up nearly to her elbow. She looked away. Her throat moved as she swallowed. Neither of us said anything. It was like we were suddenly shy with each other, which didn't make sense at all. It was awkward. Nice, but awkward.

Colonel Chipelski banged through the door then, breaking the mood. She stood at the foot of our beds with her arms crossed, glaring down at us, threatening to send us to jail if we ever—ever—*ever*—told anyone about what had happened at Imre's house, which she called the "facility in question." She had papers for us to sign to make it all official. She didn't mention Imre at all. She didn't use the words *zombie* or *zomboy*. When I asked about them, she said there were none—no zombies, no scientists, no experiment.

"No zombies at all?" I asked. "Not even one?"

The colonel had thick glasses and short hair, and talked like she had just swallowed a forkful of barbed wire. We signed. Evil-O couldn't hold the paper straight with her broken arm, so the colonel held it for her.

"You know," I said, as the colonel was getting ready to go, "Dr. Bernstein said a funny thing. Remember, Evil-O? He said the experiment had failed *again*."

Colonel Chipelski froze.

"How many experiments have there been?" I asked. "Does the army have a camp full of zombies somewhere—

results of other nuclear disasters or weird infections? Is there a plan to turn them into soldiers? Because that's a cool idea. Imre would be a great soldier. He's strong as a truck, can't be killed, follows the rules. And he never got mad, not even when the protesters were calling him names."

Evil-O was considering it. "An army of zomboys! Wow."

Colonel Chipelski waved her arms in the air. "Stop! Stop talking now! You must never speak like this again. Either of you!"

"What do you mean? I'm just imagining," I said. "Like, *what if*, you know? My official position is that there are no zombies."

(You heard me. Any zombie or zomboy I've talked about in this story? I was just making it up.)

CHAPTER 46

I GUESS IT ENDS HERE FOR NOW

Our Halloween costumes were wrecked. Our parents brought normal clothes for us to change into. They met us in the waiting room. It was pretty cool. Mom and Dad cried. Well, Dad did. Mom is tougher. Evil-O's mom was there, and she cried too.

"My daughter a hero," she said. "Imagine! I know I'm not supposed to talk about it but here you are in black-and-white." She held out a sheet of paper with an official army seal and letters spelling EVIL-O FORESTER. There was one with my name on it too.

We all drove home in my parents' car. We stopped for food on the 401. It was five in the morning. I have never enjoyed a hamburger more. Never.

||||

That was a couple of months ago. A few things have happened since then. Imre's place, which had burned to the ground, is fenced off now, and the land is for sale. The fire was written up in the newspapers as a mystery and a tragedy claiming the lives of promising young men. That's what they called Luther and RJ—*promising*. There was even a funeral. I didn't go. I never found out whose bikes we took, or what happened to them.

The army tidied up after itself and I never heard anything more about Dr. Bernstein or Dr. Miller. Or Imre. I kind of thought that the TV guys would care about him, but after a few days without any news or sightings they stopped showing up. I haven't seen his picture in weeks. The CBC special has not aired yet, and there's nothing about it on the website.

The zomboy videos are gone from YouTube, but Rappin' ZED is pretty popular. You can download a bunch of Mrs. Stinson's stuff if you want to, which I do not.

Susan Berdit switched schools. Calvin's dad got transferred, so Calvin's gone too. Andrew is class president.

I had a checkup the other day. Dr. Sophie made me take a deep breath and then blow into a tube and see how long I could keep a little ball floating in air. She said I did great.

"So my asthma's getting better," I said.

"You don't have asthma, Bob. You never did. You're fine."

She shooed me out of the office.

Evil-O's cast is off and she's doing push-ups to strengthen her left arm.

ACKNOWLEDGMENTS

Thanks to Tim and Ken, who read an early version of this story and gave me much-needed encouragement. Thanks to Hadley Dyer, who saw it patiently (there's a word) through a number of redrafts. Special thanks to Olive Loewen Marek, who sometimes signs her name backwards.